Also By Joe Moore

The Santa Claus Trilogy

Believe Again, The North Pole Chronicles
1st Book in the Trilogy

Faith, Hope & Reindeer
2nd Book in the Trilogy

Glaciers Melt & Mountains Smoke
3rd Book in the Trilogy

Santa's Elf Series©

Santa's World, Introducing Santa's Elf Series
Jamie Hardrock, Chief Mining Elf
Shelley Wrapitup, Master Design Elf

RETURN OF THE BIRDS

by

Joe Moore

Published by
The North Pole Press

Published by The North Pole Press

Smoky Mountains, Tennessee

ISBN13:978-0-9787129-9-0

Cover design by Mary Moore

This is a work of fiction. Names, characters, places and incidents are either the product of the author's imagination or are used fictitiously, and any resemblance to actual persons living or dead, companies and business establishments, events or locales is entirely coincidental or used in a fictitious manner.

Information about and for this book may be obtained through contacting North Pole Press at: Info@thenorthpolepress.com.
Printed in the United States of America

Dedication:

This book would not exist if it had not been for the genius that is Sir Alfred Hitchcock. I remember seeing The Birds shortly after its 1964 release. I have seen it several times since then, and it has always left a big impression on me. To say it "loosely" followed the original short story by Daphne du Maurier is an understatement, and after reading her story, I think mine walks the fine line between them both.

So I invite all those who needed answers from the movie, or the short story, that were never answered to finally learn what was behind it all and how it ends. But to Sir Alfred Joseph Hitchcock, KBE, dubbed "The Mystery of Suspense" I thank you for your inspiration and all the entertainment you have given me, and so very many other people.

I hope my readers find a modicum of your whispers into my ear.

Acknowledgment

This book is meant as a continuation of, and an answer to, the horror film directed by Alfred Hitchcock, which was loosely based on the 1952 story "The Birds" by Daphne du Maurier. This movie had a profound impact on me, but I always felt cheated that many of the questions from the plot never were answered.

Thankfully, I am now able to finish the tale and answer all the questions I had because of my fertile and active imagination (and with the help of the internet), and share the "rest of the story" with you.

This book was in my head even as I wrote *Faith, Hope & Reindeer* (my first novel) in 2005. It was meant to be my second book, but became my fourth after I finished the **Santa Claus Trilogy**. After ten years of rolling it around in my head, I am proud to finally put this story into your hands.

As with any book that is even remotely based on fact, a good deal of information was based on research done with the Center for Disease Control, Wikipedia, WebMD, and Medicinenet.com. The research for the viruses discussed and their vaccines came primarily from Vaccines.gov, and again the CDC.

Of course the possibility of birds developing the condition I describe in this book is almost beyond remote. But the fact of them spreading or causing the spread of disease is both factual and historic. While certain events mentioned in this book are indeed historical, I do not profess to draw any conclusions, or even summations between the events of this book and actual events. This is a work of fiction and the events I have drawn upon are of my own making.

As with all my books, I have had some great help with this and wish to thank my beta readers and those who have assisted in the polishing of this story into the shiny gem you read today. The most important of these is my editor and the man who is given me a great deal of his time and energy, along with his 40 years of journalism experience, Gary Brown. This story reads well solely due to his efforts. Second is a lady who has become a good friend. Ashley Snipes, I cannot thank her enough for all her encouragement, suggestions and assistance. This book has a lot of your touches in it, and for that I am truly grateful. Other people who have really helped out on this project are: Mary Johnson, President of Web Site Helper, LLC, Terry Reinitz, and a name I have brought up many times before, my friend and almost always gets my rough draft and helps so much, Tracy Lewis Sheppard. Thank you all for your honest comments and suggestions.

PROLOGUE

The corpse looked like it had been through a meat grinder. Except for the bloodied blue jean shorts, everything else had been ripped open and the body underneath butchered. There were parts of organs overflowing the body, and the face and extremities ripped to shreds.

The police captain had not seen anything like this. He came up through the ranks in some pretty nasty areas, but nothing as ghastly as this. Especially not in this sleepy seaside resort. Things like this didn't happen here.

He could see that the victim hadn't been shot. There were no bullet wounds when he looked. There were none of the usual knife wounds. Although there must have been some sharp implement to do this much damage, no bruising or apparent head trauma, nothing indicating foul play. But there he lies, or the remains of him, so something attacked, killed and butchered him.

Answers would come easier once he got the teenager to the morgue. Nothing more would be learned here. As he started to turn to head back to the attendants waiting to take the remains, his deputy asked him what he thought happened.

CHAPTER 1 – DAY 1

It all began with Sebastian. He was a happy bird, an expensive Cockatoo that had been presented to the Edwards family many years ago. It was a token of appreciation for all they had done for their community. Transported from a pet store in San Francisco he arrived at the city council in San Clemente, California.

Sebastian was an essential part of the family for many decades and over a couple of generations. He had always been content to sit on his perch and loved to get treats from the various family members. Unbeknownst to anyone in the Edwards' household, Sebastian was born with a strange anomaly that was similar to a common disease with many mammals. But being the carrier, he never displayed any symptoms. The fact was, Sebastian had never been sick a day in his life. However, before coming to San Clemente, he did contaminate a pair of love birds when his food tray was switched with the other bird's tray by mistake. Those birds created an extensive pandemic in Bodega Bay, California when they were purchased by a young woman to impress a man she fancied. But that story was already told. Even if never understood or investigated properly as to what caused that problem.

Sebastian lived a long and happy life. He had always been an attentive bird and never once bit or tried to bite anyone. But he began to show his age at 60. The bird was not moving very well, molted frequently, and was becoming cranky with pain. When he finally passed at 62, his family was more relieved than bereft. By then they had been waiting patiently for his inevitable end. Since they loved Sebastian, they decided to make a special place for him in their garden. So they wrapped him in an antique linen cloth and placed him in the garden behind the runaculas. They thought he would enjoy the annual blooms and felt it fitted his years of status as their family pet.

Unlike Sebastian, Boomer never really belonged to anyone. This dog was a mixed breed of sheepdog with Labrador Retriever and was a large, mostly white, fun-loving animal. He had lost his family a couple of weeks after he was brought home, little more than a puppy when he ran away and became permanently displaced. He became a feral dog but was so good-natured that many people left out scraps for him and made sure water was always available. Everyone called him Boomer because on the rare occasion when he barked, you could hear him for blocks.

A couple of days after Sebastian's ceremony in the backyard, Boomer was doing his usual neighborhood trot when he caught the whiff of something. Even from a distance dogs have a sense of smell far more acute than the most sensitive person. He entered the Edwards' backyard and loped over to Sebastian's grave. He immediately dug up the bird and complete with the linen wrappings took off with his prize to his favorite hiding spot.

That place was an open field, which was part of another home that had been for sale for about a year and a half, and left unattended for nearly as long. Boomer unwrapped and played with his new found toy for a while. He thought about eating the bird, as he had done so many times before, but he had just received a good meal of scraps from the lovely lady up the street. So after nibbling at his prize, he decided he should save this treat for later. Feeling restless and wanting to continue exploring again, Boomer reburied the bird in a hastily dug shallow pit and covered it with dirt pushed by his nose.

An hour after Boomer left, a shadow came over Sebastian's remains. Moments later it crossed the body again. After a few more times, the owner of the shadow landed at the scarcely covered bird in the ground. The female turkey vulture began picking at the carcass, and soon the feathers were spread all over. The vulture saw Boomer coming back and knew a confrontation would be inevitable and moreover, she would lose. As the final remains were small enough to carry in her beak, the giant bird decided to take the remains of Sebastian to her nest where she had several young.

It was spring, and a good many birds were hatching their first broods and food was needed to feed the hatchlings in ever-increasing amounts. This pair of vultures had three young, and they were all hungry.

The gray down-covered young vultures still needed to be mostly fed by their mother. With her help, the brood made short work of the cockatoo, and soon nothing was left but a few bones and feathers. Those were thrown to the ground and were being picked over by crows and other birds trying to gain anything from the meager pickings. That was the end of Sebastian, but the beginning of everything else.

Several days later, the mother turkey vulture began to battle her mind between the instinct to feed her young, and the need to conquer her unending desire to feed herself. Soon her mate also started becoming more voracious in his appetite. When the young vultures were just two months old, the male had already moved off in his constant search for food. The female, who was continuously feeding, had began the extraordinary practice of searching farther and farther from the nest to get enough food for herself and her fledglings.

She was also more brazen in taking meals from the road and took significant risks of being struck by cars. Had it not been for her large size and the fact she was easily seen, she might not have lasted after those first few foraging days.

Her young seemed to have no end of needing to be fed, either. They consumed every last morsel she brought. As they began flying around, they increased their territory and went far beyond what would be the reasonable behavior to gain food. That was how it all started.

CHAPTER 2 – DAY 5

Andy had lived on the beach for the past three years. At 63 his needs were few, and he had almost forgotten what it was like to have his own home or a regular bed on which to sleep. People around town knew him and would slip him a dollar or two once in a while. He stood about 5 feet 10 inches and weighed 180 pounds with dark brown curly hair. He never could grow facial hair like most men, so rarely did he look like he was unkempt as many did living off the land in San Clemente.

The authorities didn't bother Andy since he never caused any trouble. Because of the beautiful weather and scenery, the numbers of the homeless showing up was on the rise. Trying to run them off or get rid of them all was becoming an impossible situation.

Occasionally they would load some of the hapless onto the train and try to disburse them to other parts of Southern California. More often than not they would return to their pristine beaches and would retake their residence in the area. There were shelters around that would help feed them from time to time, and every Thanksgiving they would offer a bounty and pack up food in bags for them to live off of for a short while.

Most lived in the area near North Beach, a place that afforded good hiding and cover during storms. Andy had lived there for his first year, but moved further south to avoid the "crowds" that were ever increasing in that area. It had become even more heavily patrolled in recent times, as the city wanted to make sure the people wouldn't loot or vandalize the expensive homes and property sharing the beach.

He had found a hillside that was sheltered from the winds blowing off the ocean and provided an excellent cover. It was also close enough to the trash barrels that were used by restaurant patrons visiting the beach. He could watch for any leftover deposits that might help him stay fed.

Lately, he had seen an unusual sight. A giant turkey vulture had begun trying to get the barrels that were Andy's bread and butter. A couple of times he had run down to chase the bird off. Vultures were easily scared off, and one rarely saw this bird in a populated area. This one had pulled out food several times, and before Andy could chase him off, the bird had dropped the food onto the sand and ruined it for Andy.

After that, the food was only good for the seagulls hanging around, so they got the spoils of what might have been a decent handout. Seagulls were opportunists and always looking for an edible treat. They were far more aggressive in their pursuits than almost any other bird and had been a nuisance to beach visitors for ages. Given half a chance they would steal food from picnics or bags of snacks.

Lately, Andy thought the gulls had gotten worse. They seemed to steal food at a much higher rate, and he even witnessed a gull attack a man who was trying to eat a sandwich the other day. He got scratched up pretty badly from two of the aggressive gulls. But Andy guessed the man was more surprised and shocked rather than injured.

Other unwanted visitors newly seen were the crows that had taken up residence of late. Andy used to see one occasionally, but now more were appearing with regularity. It seemed that as the gulls were coming from the sea in more significant numbers, as were the crows from inland.

Pigeons rounded out the majority of the winged pests. They mostly stayed on the pier, but again began hanging closer to food sources. Andy laughed to himself and thought, *I always knew this place would go to the birds*. Andy did enjoy watching the pelicans glide across the surf, and these were the only birds he thought were worthy of being around this beautiful coastal community. Those birds he could watch for hours and had even approached a few while they rested on the pier.

After a day of foraging and walking along the beach, Andy went back to his shelter under the bluff and settled in as the golden sun began to turn crimson, sinking slowly into the sea. Another perfect day in San Clemente was coming to a close.

Sometime during the night, Andy had a terrible dream. He was being attacked by a policeman trying to drive him from his home on the beach. But instead of using guns, they were using a cattle prod and sharpened sticks. They kept jabbing him on his right side pushing him toward the sea. His ribs were getting wet from the surf, and though he continued fighting the officers off, new ones kept coming with more prods and they would stick him again and again.

Finally, Andy woke to a sight more terrifying than his nightmare concocted. The giant turkey vulture sat atop Andy, poking at his side with his beak. The bird had urinated on Andy as it was tearing at him. It had broken the skin, and an ugly wound was leaking blood onto his shirt and pants. Andy screamed and threw the bird off him. The vulture took off and was gone before Andy could do anything to it. He couldn't believe what had happened and almost went into shock from the incident. Andy searched for help, but the beach was barren. He went up to the center of the village and began going up Avenida Del Mar, which ran down the center of the town until he finally saw a police car.

He flagged the patrol car down, and when the officer on the right side lowered his window, Andy started yelling about how a giant bird attacked him. The officer shook his head and said, "Look, buddy, why don't you go home or wherever you stay and sleep it off."

Andy protested to the officer further and showed him the wound the bird inflicted. The cop and his partner guessed that Andy was drunk and most likely fell and cut himself. He stunk terribly, and both officers figured that Andy wanted them to tend to him and let him stay the night at the station. The closest patrolman wrinkled his nose and told Andy to back away from the car.

Andy stepped back but continued his protestations. The car pulled away as if he wasn't even there. Andy yelled a few obscenities at the disappearing car, but the sheriff's deputies ignored him and continued on their way. Realizing no help was coming tonight, Andy thought he better tend to his cuts himself for fear of becoming infected. Andy could barely stand his stench where the bird soiled him. He went into the public restroom on the beach and wet his shirt to begin cleaning the injuries. The wound was a nasty gouge about 6 inches long and was more profound than first realized. He reckoned another inch or so and his innards would be outwards.

It took about 15 minutes to wash off the blood and hold the wound with his shirt until the blood clotted, Andy again smelled the strong odor of ammonia from his pants and began pouring water from the sink down his leg. At first, his efforts made the smell even worse, and he thought he might get sick from the stench. The man finally removed his pants and soaked them in the sink until the foul smell dissipated. He was already cold and figured it would take all night for his pants to dry enough to keep him warm, but at least he no longer reeked from the bird.

When he emerged from the bathroom, he looked around expecting to see the bird again. He wondered if his enclave would be safe and looked around for a more reliable haven with which to rest. He decided to relax where the park came close to the railroad tracks on a bench. Although concerned about the openness where he laid, he felt it would be easy to spot any approaching predators.

The vulture was again on the hunt. He was cruising up and down the Interstate 5 highway and looking around the Pacific Coast Highway and surrounding roads. There was almost always roadkill near one of the highways, and he had been cruising these streets more often than he ever did before. Got to eat. Got to eat. It was the only thing on his mind. Long gone was his mate, his brood, and his other companions.

This vulture used to spend long lazy days hanging around the electrical towers in San Juan Capistrano with dozens of his companions. Each day, one by one they would take flight and begin riding the thermals higher and higher until they were almost impossible for the human eye to see. For hours they would hover taking one warm current after another, as they searched the landscape for an easy meal. It needed to be far from danger, away from traffic, and utterly dead to the point of decomposing. If the bird could smell it, then it was ripe for the taking.

Now he sought out anything that wasn't moving. The other day he had found a small injured dog, and while the dog tried to bite him, his sharp beak bashed through its head and stopped the animal from moving. He tore at it in big chunks. He preferred meat long dead, but would now feed on anything he could find. Got to eat. Got to eat.

He saw others of his kind were beginning to take up the night foraging as he had done. A couple of these he noticed were from his old nesting area. He didn't visit this area anymore as it no longer meant anything to

him, only his need for food, from which he rarely
wavered. Once in a while, he would perch in a high tree
or a telephone pole, but mostly his hunger drove him to
fly continuously.

He spotted a dead opossum on a side road up ahead.
It looked like another of his kind had gotten there first.
He landed short of the dead animal and began to
approach. Got to eat. Got to eat. GOT TO EAT! The
other bird began grunting and flaring out its wings.
Ordinarily, this would have caused the intruder to hold
off, but this bird came instead and started grabbing
anything in front of it.

The other bird tried to fend off the newcomer and
spread its wings full, but the vulture kept taking beak
fulls of anything it could grab. The first vulture decided
that the only way to determine this was to eat as much
of the remains as it could ahead of this unwanted guest.
The two birds grabbed chunks of the animal until there
was scarcely a bone or patch of fur left.

High above another bird watched the interaction but
decided there was not enough left from the one animal
to challenge the vultures below. This bird was another
that rarely, if ever, did nocturnal flights. It was a Red-
tailed hawk, and unlike the vultures, the hawk could
attack other animals and was well equipped to do so.

CHAPTER 3 – DAY 6

The next morning Andy was trying to tell a lifeguard about last night's incident. The lifeguard was Chris Palmer, and Andy had spoken to him many times before. Chris stood about six foot one and was a handsome man, even by lifeguard standards. He had steel blue eyes and brown hair that felt even softer than it looked. He always kept it combed to one side. The guard listened to the man and looked at the wound under his shirt. He winced a bit and said, "Andy that looks nasty has anyone looked at that?"

Chris pulled out his first aid box, and Andy let him administer some antiseptic cream and bandage the wound. Chris suggested Andy see a doctor about it, but Andy shrugged and said he would be fine.

"Chris, I tried to tell the cops, but they acted like I was drunk or something and practically rolled over my toes to get away from me," Andy explained, "Thanks for your help. That's probably all I needed."

"I gotta tell you, man, I have never heard of a bird attacking anyone, in their sleep or otherwise. Are you sure it wasn't a nightmare?" asked Chris suspiciously.

"I'm tellin' you," insisted Andy, "In fact, I was having a nightmare that the police were after me until I woke to find Birdzilla on me! He bit the crap outta me and pissed all over my clothes."

"You know there's a gal in town that perhaps you could talk to," Chris said, "She's studying to be an ornithologist and is up here from the Wild Animal Park studying seabird migration. She's working on a project for the park and the San Diego Zoo."

"She's a what?" asked Andy.

"She studies birds," said Chris, "She's going to be around for a few more weeks observing pelicans and other seabirds during their breeding season."

"Yeah? I hope she knows what is going on around here. Have you seen all the damn birds hangin' around now? Look at all the damn things," Andy spat as he looked and pointed at the gulls.

"Probably no more than usual," commented Chris, "After all, it is the mating season, and they're all out looking for a piece of tail."

"Yeah, well I wouldn't mind scrambling up a few omelets with their eggs after last night," Andy growled, "When they start attacking me, all's fair after that."

Chris tried to settle the man down. Being a third-year lifeguard, he knew many of the homeless people that hung on the beach. The lifeguard met Andy his first year on the job and always liked the man. Andy rarely was upset like he was now. He mostly was jovial and even would kid Chris about the female tourists that flocked to the sand and his lifeguard chair every year.

"All these damn women want is your hard body out of those red shorts," Andy would tease him and often say that they would serve him up on a plate if he would let them.

Andy liked Chris as well and thought he was one of the more tolerant and easy going of the guards. He figured some of them had their shorts too tight and it cut off blood to their brains making them either mean or stupid, and sometimes both. Many acted like Andy had chosen this nomadic life on the beach and that he could afford any one of the multimillion-dollar homes on the sand at his whim.

Chris said to Andy that he would talk with Tory when next he saw her and ask her to meet him.

"You need to hang around here where I can find you," said Chris, "I don't want her thinking I'm sending her on a wild goose chase."

"Let's leave the stupid bird analogies out of this, okay?" grumbled Andy, "So you like this gal? I get it. I'll be at your beck and call."

Chris just chuckled and ignored Andy's observation.

Later that morning Chris saw Tory McKnight carrying a cup and her notebook. She was in her usual outfit of khaki cargo shorts and a green scooped-neck shirt with teal overshirt hanging open to the breeze.

He had run into her one morning at the local coffee shop while in line. She noticed his red jacket and shorts and asked if he was a lifeguard. After they got their orders, since the place was full, she invited him to join her at one of the smaller tables to the side. She was a pretty lady about the same age that he was. She wore her cinnamon color hair down to the middle of her back and permed with tight curls. She had hazel eyes, a few freckles and a little mole below her lip on the left side of her face.

He learned about her study program and that she is working with the zoology department. She was getting her masters degree and planned to get a doctorate in ornithology from San Diego State University. She then hoped to get a permanent position at either the Wild Animal Park or San Diego Zoo.

Ever since that morning, each day Chris watched to see her working at the pier. He had a hard time concentrating on the swimmers, rather than spying on her. She noticed him in the guard stand and waved to him. He beckoned her over and saw she changed direction.

A few moments later she came up to his stand and asked, "And how is the protector of the waves this fine morning?"

Chris laughed and returned, "Just dandy, and how is Ms. Ornithologist?"

She did a mock curtsy and said, "I'm fine, thank you for asking, so what's going on?"

Chris answered, "Funny you should ask, have you ever heard of birds attacking people?"

The smile left her face, and she scowled saying, "Only extremely rarely. It would be about as common as a lion walking down this beach."

Chris sighed and said, "Yeah, I kinda thought so, but I got this guy..."

That moment Andy came jogging up and out of breath asked Chris, "Is this her? Is this the bird lady?"

Chris gave a look of apology to Tory and said to

Andy, "Andy this is Tory McKnight, the future ornithologist."

She looked at Andy and said, "How do you do Andy. Yes, I'm the bird lady." She couldn't help but grin as she said this.

"Hey doc, I need to talk to you about a buzzard that attacked me," Andy began at once.

"Uh, I'm sorry I didn't get that," she just stared at him, "What kind of buzzard, and how did it attack you?"

Andy began his tale of how he was asleep when the turkey vulture started pecking at him during the night. In the end, he asked, "Is there something wrong with that damn bird?"

Tory started pushing the sand around with her right foot and bit her lip. She eventually looked up and said with a very straight face to Andy, "I'll have to look into this. Could you do me a favor, I can't act on this information until I see the bird close up. Could you alert me when you see this bird again?"

Andy nodded and said, "Well I gotta tell ya miss, I hope I don't see him again, but if I do I will point him out at once, except they all look the same to me. A big black buzzard with an ugly redhead hopping around the beach, can't miss it."

"Thank you, Andy. Now if you would excuse me, there is something I need to talk to Chris about right now."

"Oh, sure," Andy grinned, "I won't get in the way of the mating season here, heh, heh." Andy turned and walked away.

Tory turned back to Chris, and he asked, "So? Is there anything to his story?"

Tory looked disgusted and said, "God, what are they drinking on this beach? That guy is totally and completely off his rocker."

"So there's no chance of any truth to his tale?" Chris sounded disappointed.

"Not a shred. First off vultures are the most docile and easily spooked bird species. And they aren't buzzards, that term relates to hawks. Vultures wouldn't get near anything that was moving no matter how hungry they were, or how many young they had to feed." Tory's nose began to flare, "Second, those birds can't attack anything as they have no talons and can't carry anything with their feet, which are very sensitive. Moreover, their necks and beaks aren't large enough to carry anything much bigger than a mouthful."

"Whoa, calm down Tory," Chris said defensively, "I just hoped you could straighten him out about this. Could it have been a gull or crow or something else that he just thought was a vulture?"

"He's not right in the head. None of the birds you mentioned forage at night, and they don't attack people either unless you were disturbing a nest or harassing the birds in some way," she said shaking her head.

"He was saying that there are more birds here than usual, and I have to agree with him. They seem everywhere this year, is there a possibility there is too much competition for food and that more of them are coming here?" Chris asked.

"Some years more birds migrate back and forth than other years. Most of the birds around here are year round and don't fly off," Tory explained, "Maybe they are congregating differently than in years past, but they have been here and will remain here in roughly the same numbers as before."

"Well something got to him, and I have to say he's carrying a nasty gash on his side," Chris added.

"He probably was drinking and landed on a rock wrong when he fell," Tory said with contempt.

"Hang on Tory, there are a lot of homeless people here, but I've not known Andy to be a drunk, or have I ever seen him drinking," Chris was a little upset and let her know it. "These people have nothing left but their reputation, and I've never known Andy to make wild claims or exaggerations about anything. Come to think of it; this is the first time I've ever heard him utter a complaint."

"Okay, I'm sorry to be judgmental, but there is no way a turkey vulture or any other kind of bird attacked him," she said more softly. "I guess I am a little defensive about my winged creatures."

"Has any bird ever attacked a human with the intent to cause serious harm?" questioned Chris.

"Not for more than 50 years, and that was an isolated instance, and it was never really discovered why," she said, "The birds all died out and no study was ever done to reveal anything unusual. Unfortunately, the people attacked couldn't say too much about it either."

"Was it like that bird flu thing in Asia?" Chris asked.

"I don't think so, besides the bird flu virus is a recent problem and not anything that we aren't getting under control," Tory answered in a matter-of-fact tone.

"Well since my sneaky plan of asking you out to dinner to discuss this disturbing report has failed, I guess I will have to ask you without a pretense. How about dinner sometime this week?" Chris asked then held his breath.

Tory laughed out loud, "You felt you needed a pretense? Do I seem that unapproachable? Yes, dinner would be lovely. How about tomorrow night? I have to take care of some things tonight."

"That sounds great. Where do I pick you up?" he said letting his breath out.

"I am staying with a family in this neighborhood," she said while she scribbled in her notebook, "This is the address and why don't we say 7 tomorrow."

"I'll be there," he grinned, "Now I need to get back to work, I might have lost several swimmers by now."

"Yeah, and meanwhile an entire species just passed by that I needed to catalog," she chuckled.

She turned and began to walk away. Chris had trouble looking toward the surf.

On the southern part of town was another park owned by the state. It was a rocky outcropping that had a variety of shallow caves and enclaves. This area had also been a refuge for a few of the homeless occasionally, but an even more significant hangout for teenagers. They would bring their illegal drugs and alcohol to this area and hide out from everyone else. They made small fire pits and drank or pass their drugs under the stars until they either went home or passed out.

It was also known for its nudity as the sheriff's deputies couldn't see the beach from the parking lot, and many never left their cars while patrolling. This area was the most extensive retreat for first-time skinny-dipping adventures that were mostly harmless. However, a few teenage pregnancies started on that beach, too.

Weekends were the worst for these illicit activities, but some weeknights had seen a few of these parties, as the weekend was so crowded in spring and summer. This week had pleasant temperatures in the high 60's, and the kids were feeling a little restless after the chilly days of the last several weeks.

A few of the young people decided to visit the south rocks, as they are called, and had met up about 7 that evening. Greg had brought some firewood and charcoal, Tommy brought "refreshments" as he called them, and the others came with either snacks or nothing. There were eight in total, five boys and three girls. They began passing around the two bottles Tommy brought, and after a short period, the tongues came loose along with some of the clothing. A couple of the guys were hitting on the girls and Tommy was holding court, complaining about his life in San Clemente.

John, one of the other guys started asking Tommy what his problem was, "Shit man, you got two of everything, two big houses with pools, two sets of parents, a couple of cars. Everything you ask for you get from your folks."

"My parents are losers," Tommy argued, "They come home at night and have a few cocktails before dinner, talk bullshit about their fucking jobs during dinner and pass out in front of the TV. They pay no attention to my sister or me. They drink so damn much that they don't ever even notice when I take their booze."

"Well," said John, "At least you got parents, I only have my old lady, and she works two jobs to keep us living in that shithole of an apartment we're in."

Tommy went on talking about his sad state of affairs as a wealthy son to a son-of-a-bitch father, who he was convinced had to be reminded of his own son's name. John told him he was starting to slur his words and should knock off the Canadian Club. Tommy waved him off and then gave him the finger when John tried to insist.

John said he was heading home and a few others watching the exchange got up with him. The two couples that had shown interest in one another had already left to find a quieter stretch of sand below the outcropping.

Tommy now sat by himself, poking the dying fire and drinking the whiskey. He was all right with his private pity party and cursed his friends for not caring any more than his parents. Fuck 'em, the boy thought to himself. He began to get sleepy and decided it might be time for him to head home, but he couldn't seem to move. The liquor had already done its work.

As he upended the last of the bottle he held, he fell over on his back and passed out. Something watched the entire event unfold. To the hawk perched on the bluff above, it looked like Tommy was going through his last death throws. This would be an easy meal. Got to eat. Got to eat. GOT TO EAT!

Once the bird was sure the boy was dead, he swooped out over the rocks and circled for a while, watching and waiting. He was impatient to get to his prey. He finally landed next to the boy's shoulder and neck and eyed the passed out kid. With a lucky strike, his sharp beak severed the carotid artery. Tommy's eyes popped open. He grabbed his neck. It was too late. The last thing he saw was a yellow eye looking into his green one, and then Tommy passed out again, this time for good.

Before long, as the hawk was feeding voraciously, seagulls began showing up and trying to take morsels from the hawk's meal. He tried fighting them off at first, but the body was too large to covet the whole thing. More large birds fell from the sky and before dawn the next day, much of the boy was gone. New birds came in the early morning and picked up where the others had left off. It was easy pickings now as so much damage had been done during the night. If not for his school ID, he would not have been able to be identified from his remains.

CHAPTER 4 – DAY 7

They didn't find the boy until the following afternoon, and it was his friend John who came looking for him after he didn't show up in school. When the sheriff's car pulled up to the area, the deputies started pushing people back. John was retching off to the side and crying uncontrollably. Deputy Jerry Collinswood's partner, Deputy Bob Williams, went to John, while Deputy Collinswood checked out the crime scene.

"Jesus H. Christ," he said looking at the corpse. It looked to Deputy Collinswood that the body had been through a meat grinder. Already the crabs were picking at the few scraps underneath the body. He pushed a couple away and spoke into his radio. "Yeah, this is Deputy Collinswood, we need the coroner at this location, and have him hurry." He listened to the response and said, "No, this one is dead, no medics needed."

After he turned back to the gathering crowd, he told everyone to leave the area that this was now a crime scene and closed to the public until they could figure out what happened.

A second sheriff's car pulled up. Deputy Collinswood recognized the occupants as Deputy Ann Hernandez and Deputy Gil Dodge. They left the car and came closer. Deputy Collinswood asked Deputy Hernandez to help Deputy Williams get a statement from the kid over there, while he and Deputy Dodge kept the curiosity seekers from getting too close.

"So what is it? One of our homeless drop dead?" asked Deputy Dodge.

"I don't think this one dropped dead, and judging from his clothes I don't think he was a homeless person," Deputy Collinswood said in a low breath, "It looks like this one was ripped to shreds by something."

Deputy Dodge looked at Deputy Collinswood and said, "What we have werewolves on the beach now?"

"Not funny, Gil. Go look for yourself," said Deputy Collinswood.

Deputy Dodge walked up to the crevice and looked in, "Good Christ," was all he said. He moved closer and looked at the remains. The eyes were missing, and the flesh torn from the face, arms, and chest. The victim looked disemboweled. Similarly, there was little left of the legs except for bones. He walked back to Deputy Collinswood and said, "Shit, how long has he been lying there?"

"According to the kid he just came up missing this morning," answered Deputy Collinswood.

"That's impossible," Deputy Dodge protested, "No way. Too much damage for that short of time. Christ, there's nothing left to him. Maybe he thinks that was his friend and it's someone else," Deputy Dodge finished.

"He told Bob he and some friends were in that very place last evening and he built a fire they sat around," explained Deputy Collinswood, "I think they would have noticed a corpse sitting around the fire with them."

"So what do you think, a dog? Shit, that looks like a cougar got to it," Deputy Dodge was still reeling from the sight. Nothing like this ever took place in San Clemente. The most he usually responded to was domestic violence and nuisance calls.

"We'll know soon enough, here comes the wagon now," Deputy Collinswood pointed to the Coroner's vehicle pulling up to the area. Followed by the lieutenant of his division, who was also the chief of police for the city. He and sheriff's deputy Dodge cleared a path for the cars and put it as close as they could get it to the rocks.

"Right up here, lieutenant," deputy Collinswood led the way as the attendants pulled out the gurney. The lieutenant asked the attendants to wait a moment while he took a look and determined the cause of death.

The lieutenant and deputy Collinswood walked up to the body, and the lieutenant said nothing as he examined the remains. After a few minutes deputy Collinswood asked, "Any ideas?"

"Never seen anything like it," Lieutenant Joe Ferguson said, "We don't even see them like this when they have decomposed for weeks. And this is fresh, perhaps no more than 15 to 20 hours old. We will know more when we get him back and let the medical examiner inspect the damage."

"Do you think it was a feral dog or something?"

deputy Collinswood pressed.

"These don't look like bite marks," the lieutenant said rubbing his thinning hair, "It almost looks like someone took a knife or something and just butchered the guy. And there doesn't seem to be many organs left."

He stood up and asked Deputy Collinswood, "Did you see any other signs of blood or struggle?"

Deputy Collinswood said he did a cursory look, but then came back to keep onlookers away. The lieutenant nodded, "Well, take a look around. I can't believe there isn't something left of this guy around here somewhere.

The lieutenant signaled for the attendants to come up with the gurney. Even these pros of death were shocked and revolted at the condition of the body. They almost had to pick it up in pieces to get everything loaded. They placed the remains from head to toe, or what remained of it, into a body bag and then carefully strapped it down.

"Hey lieutenant?" Deputy Collinswood called down from up the slope. The lieutenant walked up, and Deputy Collinswood pointed to some tracks on the rocks. They were made with blood.

"That's odd. These prints look like bird tracks. I wonder if they walked across the body and just came up to the rocks. Strange," the lieutenant said merely, then turned and came back down looking around as he did so. They appeared to be around the escarpment in various places.

"Had to be more than one for all this," Deputy Collinswood thought out loud.

"Looks like huge feet or talons or whatever they call them," remarked the lieutenant, "Whatever they are, I think they must have scavenged the body and tracked it around."

"I don't see anything that looks like a fight and no other tracks of note," said Deputy Collinswood, "Maybe he just fell and busted his head or something."

"I already looked for that. And how did the body get shredded like it was?" Lieutenant Ferguson asked, "Something must have caused that damage before or immediately after, and then the birds came by later and made a mess of it. I've never known birds to do such a thorough job."

The two men looked around some more when deputy Dodge who had walked further to see if he could find anything returned. "I don't see anything suspicious looking around this place, and no animal or man-made tracks of any kind," said deputy Dodge.

"All right as soon as deputies Hernandez and Williams finish putting the tape up you guys are free," stated the lieutenant, "I'll head over to the morgue with the corpse and see if the M.E. can figure this out."

It took about another twenty minutes to post enough rebar and tape to cordon off the area, and Deputy Williams returned to the car where Deputy Collinswood was waiting. It was the subject of conversation between the two men most the rest of that day.

ᴋᴋᵗᴋ ᴋᴋᵗᴋ ᴋᴋᵗᴋ ᴋᵗ ᴋᴋᵗᴋ ᴋᴋᵗᴋ ᴋᴋᵗᴋ

Chris Palmer had been anxious all day about his date. He didn't date much as most of the girls around San Clemente were just a little too young, or were tourists and not hanging around long enough to make them attractive.

When he first spoke with Tory, he suspected that the second reason would be the case as well. In for a day or two and then gone again, but when she said she lived not far from the Wild Animal Park and would be here for several weeks, it piqued his interest. Not to mention she was both pretty and smart.

He planned to take her to Rosario's, one of the better Italian restaurants in the area. News traveled quickly up and down the shore about the young man found dead in the South Beach area. He heard another lifeguard say news reports thought it was a massive animal attack and that birds were also involved.

Chris thought this interesting after Andy's earlier complaint. But he knew better than to mention this to Tory as her hackles would raise after the last time. The previous corpse they had found at the beach was a couple of years ago. One of the homeless people had died of exposure in the winter. While it never got brutally cold in Southern California, occasionally it would get down to the high 30's or 40's.

But that body was found whole, and nothing untoward happened. Before then, except for an occasional traffic accident or medical condition, no bodies were found around the town.

Chris watched out over the sea when he saw it. A

giant turkey vulture was circling over the shore and not very high up.

Chris had never seen one so close to water before. The bird was coming over the bluff and would circle over the beach and soar back over toward town again. On his third circle, Andy came running up yelling, "That's him! That's the sonofabitch that attacked me!"

Chris held up his hand to shield his eyes and said to Andy, "Are you sure? They all look alike to me, though I haven't seen one hanging around the beach so closely before."

"I'm tellin' ya," Andy fairly screamed, "That's Birdzilla! That's the one that took a chunk outta me. Shoot him!"

Chris laughed at Andy and said, "Uh, they don't give us guns, and I'm pretty sure that discharging one on a public beach would land me in jail and the bird would go free and unhurt."

"But that's him!" Andy was still yelling even though Chris tried to calm him down.

"I believe you, but until it either lands or attacks someone else, there is not very much I can do about it," Chris said calmly.

"How about a cop? You have got a radio. Why don't you call a cop and let him shoot the damn thing before it takes a bite outta someone else?" Andy insisted.

"Again, I think it is even against the law for a cop to shoot his gun without a much better reason than you think that's the bird that pecked you," Chris answered reasonably.

"Pecked me? What do you mean pecked me? He tried to eat me like a hamburger!" insisted the distraught man.

They both looked up to see the bird had flown off. Chris half suspected Andy's constant yelling scared the bird off. "I guess it's gone," Chris said thankfully.

Andy looked crestfallen hoping to get revenge against the bird that tortured him that night. As they were looking around Chris noticed a young girl of about ten or eleven walking some trash from her family's picnic over to the barrel. Suddenly a seagull dove straight down and hit her with a good deal of force. The young girl cried out and dropped the trash.

A second gull hit her in the head from the other side. Before anyone could react to the second ambush, three more gulls joined the other two and began pecking at the girl, while another two landed in the trash and started ripping it apart.

Chris jumped off his stand by the time the other gulls showed up and ran to the girl's aid. As he reached her, the birds were jabbing and stabbing her, and she was bleeding from a few places. Chris started yelling and flinging his arms to chase the birds away. But they stayed close by and continued their onset until he reached her and started swatting the birds with his powerful arms.

The gulls reluctantly gave ground, but not before one of them landed a hard beak on Chris' forearm. The attack failed to draw blood. He smacked the bird hard enough to knock it to the ground, and then it hopped off and flew away.

The other birds began to break off their attack when more people including Andy, came up and started flailing arms, jackets and towels at the creatures. Finally, the last of the birds flew off, and Chris turned his attention to the girl. She was shaking violently and cut in numerous places. It was hard to see how severely she was injured because the birds had drawn a good deal of blood.

Chris began carefully dabbing at her injuries as she stood there crying. Her mother ran up and started screaming at the sight of her bloody daughter. Andy went over to her and began consoling her and trying to calm her down for the sake of her daughter, if not for herself.

When he finally had her under control, Chris sent Andy to his station to fetch the first aid kit he'd used on Andy and bring it back. Since it hadn't had much time to clot or dry, Chris was able to get most of the fresh blood wiped away with his towel. He asked the girl her name, and she answered, "Rachel" between her sobs.

"Okay Rachel," he said soothingly, "You are going to be okay. Those nasty birds are gone, and you are cleaning up fine. The scratches may hurt a bit, but I'm going to take that hurt away in a moment."

Andy returned with the first aid kit as the mother was asking Rachel why the birds attacked. Her daughter said, "They were mad at me cuz I didn't give 'em our food."

"Well," Chris said not wanting to dispute the girl's

claim, but thinking that was her naïve innocence. He finished, "They must have figured Rachel was a threat to them or something. I've seen gulls snap at people before, but not attack them like that."

"Maybe they were chums to the Birdzilla that attacked me," scoffed Andy.

Chris shot him a look that closed Andy's working mouth. The mother asked, "They attacked you, too?"

"Different time, different kind of bird," was all Andy said. Then to get out of an uncomfortable situation he told Chris he was going for some water for Rachel.

Chris said, "Please bring two glasses, one for her to drink and one to help clean these scratches." Chris knew that in truth they were cuts, but was trying to downplay the severity of the wounds.

People who helped chase off the gulls were asking others if they had ever seen such a sight, and what did they think caused it? Then Tory walked up and asked Chris what had happened. He already was dreading having to tell her about this and was hoping he wouldn't see her before dinner tonight.

Before he could answer Rachel's mother fairly yelled, "A bunch of crazed birds attacked my baby! That's what happened!"

"Well that's surprising," Tory said dumbfounded. "Did anyone else see the attack?" she asked. To which several spectators standing around began nodding their heads and answering yes. "Chris, did you see it?"

"See it?" one of the older men standing next to him said, "He chased the damned things off her. Him and some of us other folks."

Chris nodded his head and said, "It was nuts, Tory. I've never seen so many gulls go crazy all at once. Not even around the fishing boats."

She looked at him and said, "Are you both okay?"

Chris smiled at Rachel as he administered first aid ointment to the worst of the cuts and said, "Oh yeah, we're okay aren't we Rachel? Just some scratches, but I'm going to ask you to go with your Mom to the Guard Station and let's get a better look at those and find some cool bandages for them."

Rachel had quit crying by now and just nodded at Chris, "Thank you, sir," she said meekly.

"Call me Chris, Rachel," he answered with a warm smile. He spoke into his radio and advised them he was bringing an injured girl to the office for medical treatment.

The radio squawked back and acknowledged his transmission. He looked at Rachel's mother and said: "Would you come with me, please?" He was already thinking of how to word the report he was going to have to fill out on this and guessed his superiors might think him nuts.

He took the two ladies to the station. He said goodbye to Rachel and headed back to his post, the first aid kit still in his hand. He saw Tory waiting for him, and before he could set the equipment down, she asked, "So what happened, was she chasing them around the beach or throwing something at them?"

"I saw it, Tory. She was carrying their trash to the

garbage. Her hands were full, and she minded her own business, and then one gull came out of nowhere, and suddenly there were about ten. They all began pecking, first at the trash, then at the girl." He just shook his head when he finished.

"What's going on around here?" Tory asked in disbelief.

"That is not all," said Chris in a low voice.

"What do you mean?" she looked at him.

"Maybe we should discuss this at dinner," he said regretting he opened this can of worms right now.

"Oh no you don't," she gave him a wary look. "Spill it now or you will be eating alone tonight," she said half teasing.

"Well there was a young man found dead in South Park Beach and they said there were bird tracks all over the area," he said flatly.

"Are you suggesting that birds killed someone?" she looked at him incredulously.

"No! That's not what I'm saying at all. Just that they seem to be having some pretty bizarre behavior around here lately, and I was hoping you might have a theory or explanation," he said.

"I'm sure I don't because I don't know all the facts of the girl, or the young man. Maybe he'd been dead a while?" she responded.

Chris shook his head, "He was fine the night previous and was in the same spot the next afternoon but severely decomposed."

"And you think this has something to do with your

buddy's story of being attacked by a vulture?" she raised her eyebrows when she asked.

"Not necessarily, although you must admit it seems a little coincidental that three things happened in a couple of days." Chris was hoping she might agree.

"Three incidents that are wholly unrelated and I'm not at all convinced about the first or third, she said. "But maybe I'll talk to that little girl some more. What was her name?"

"Rachel," Chris answered, "I left them at the guard station, but go easy on her. She's had a bad day already."

Tory smiled at Chris and said, "I'm not THAT scary!" and walked toward the station laughing.

"Hope not," Chris murmured under his breath and began looking at the swimmers for any new trouble while at the same time, keeping one eye on the sky.

ᕁ ᕁ ᕁ ᕁ ᕁ ᕁ ᕁ ᕁ ᕁ ᕁ ᕁ ᕁ ᕁ ᕁ ᕁ ᕁ ᕁ ᕁ ᕁ

In San Juan Capistrano there was a section in the residential area along a greenbelt that was overshadowed by a string of electric towers. There were occupants at the foot of the belt in one particular tower. At every level were perched turkey vultures, as there always was in the morning and evening. It was something the residents were quite used to seeing. Sometimes there were as many as twenty-five vultures spreading and warming their wings and making it look like a giant cloak engulfed the tower. The silent vigils would watch people come and go and see the dogs around the greenbelt. There was also a small playground for young children to play nearby.

The vultures took all the activities in and would often circle high in the sky as a band. This particular afternoon one such aerial dance was taking place. About fifteen birds were circling lazily in the warm afternoon sun. It seemed aimless, but the vultures were concentrating on anything that might provide sustenance. They each had been growing more and more insatiable in their appetite. They were almost feverish in their continuous pursuit of food.

As soon as a carcass was spotted, they were on it like a swarm of Africanized honey bees. Picking every morsel clean until only the bones remained. They were taking greater risks as some of these birds couldn't wait until their meal was completely cold, and began landing on animals still in the final throws of death. Whether from natural causes, or as a result of an unplanned rendezvous with a car, the birds would swoop down as quickly as a meal presented itself.

In a twist of truly bizarre behavior, the vultures were accompanied by crows and ravens. Even a seagull or two that would move in and out of their group looking to score something to eat. The vultures, usually very social animals with their own kind, had begun grunting and snapping at each other and the other creatures around them when they lit on something. When they found a meal, they were even more aggressive and would do anything they could to keep from sharing. Now a carcass of any size would be completely covered by birds of several types and would be stripped to the bone in no time at all.

Some of the less experienced birds became meals themselves when clipped by speeding cars going up and down Pacific Coast Highway. Most of the vultures knew better and were more careful, but the crows and gulls were not used to scavenging so close to the road and flew away too late or got too close for drivers to avoid them.

There always seemed to be more to take their place, and each new meal was covered within moments of its demise.

Chris lived off one of the streets by the greenbelt in San Juan Capistrano. He and his roommate, Steve, would run the belt each day to stay in peak physical condition. Steve and Chris knew that individually they could not afford the high price of real estate in California, but they did not care to rent, either. They decided to pool resources and see if they could find a reasonable place. They found a house that came on the market that was far below its actual value. The original owner had recently passed away, and the family took a severe hit from the housing market collapse a few years before. Anxious to be rid of the property, they sold the house to Chris and Steve for about three-quarters of its appraised value.

Steve and Chris had gone through lifeguard training together, and both held jobs during the winter as paramedics. Steve was still going to medical school and was a couple of years from graduation. While Chris was

very proficient as a medic, he wasn't sure he wanted
that as his chosen vocation and was considering
becoming a doctor. He planned to continue in his
current position for two more years and re-enter college.

Chris came home after his shift and decided to go for
a run to work off his anxiety and nervousness before
getting ready for his date with Tory. Steve had been off
that day and said he had been lounging around too
much and offered to go with Chris.

It was another beautiful afternoon, and they decided
to jog the whole belt. The guys had gone about halfway
through and had come to the central part of the park.
As they ran around one of the corners they saw it. A
huge group of birds of various species in a tight group
squawking and jumping over each other. They saw that
there was an animal at the bottom of the pile. Steve
veered toward the group yelling and flailing his arms to
chase the winged creatures away. Even then, they
refused to take flight until Steve was practically on top
of them.

"It's a dog, or at least what's left of him," Steve said.
He looked at the picked-over carcass and could hardly
see any fur or markings to determine the breed.

"Wow, that's incredible," Chris said when he caught
up to his friend, "It's hard to tell what it was." Even
though Chris was a medic, he revolted at the sad shape
of the animal.

"How long do you think it has been here?" asked
Steve.

"Couldn't have been long," answered Chris, "I just

ran this yesterday, and I didn't see it here."

"I wonder what happened to it," said Steve while looking around, "It is obviously too far from the road for a car to hit it. Maybe it ran into a bigger dog and ripped it to shreds."

As he bent down to take a closer look, a crow came out of nowhere and smacked Steve square on his head. "Hey!" he yelled out and spun on the bird. He missed hitting it, and the crow flew off.

"What the hell is going on around here," Steve said as he got to his feet holding his head.

Chris looked at his roommate's head and said, "No damage. You'll live another day." But immediately Chris' thoughts went to the other incidents involving birds, including the girl on the beach, Andy, and the dead boy found on the south shore.

They left the dead dog and continued their run. Chris told him about what had been going on recently. Steve also heard about the teenager and said that they didn't seem any closer to knowing what caused the kid's death.

Steve said he had seen more activity from the birds on his watch as well, but he knew of no attacks. "That crow seemed to have it in for me," he said, "That's never happened before."

"It doesn't seem to make sense," said Chris, "I am hoping Tory can explain it."

"Oh, charming dinner conversation," Steve laughed, "Tell me is that going to be your opening line, or are you going to save that and serve it up with the main course?"

"I have a feeling she'll bring it up before I do," Chris said, "She's kinda hot on the topic, considering it's her field of study. I doubt I'm gonna dodge that bullet even if I want to, and I'm not sure I do. I'd like to know what is going on."

"Well do us both a favor and leave this little jog out of the conversation," said Steve, "I don't want to be interrogated by your new flame."

"No promises, if she begins looking at me like I should be committed, I may need to exonerate myself further with this little event," chuckled Chris, "But hopefully by then we'll be on a different topic."

"Yeah, like 'your place or mine'," teased his friend.

"It will be mine, as she is staying with another family," answered Chris with a smile, "I like this one. She doesn't seem to be too pretentious or aloof, but we'll see how things progress. She may want to feed me to the birds before dessert."

"You may want to be careful what you order for dinner, I'd avoid fowl if possible," chuckled Steve.

"And I promise I won't make any comments like 'Gee, everything tastes like chicken,'" Chris retorted.

They had already forgotten the dog, which by now was covered again with birds. Nor did they notice the flock circling above their heads directly above it.

They returned to the house, and Chris had a snack to hold him over, as it was only now approaching 4. He figured it would be about three-and-a-half hours until he ate dinner and didn't want to be so ravenous that he paid more attention to his meal than to Tory.

Once he finished his snack, he laid out what he wanted to wear that evening, then took a shower and got ready for his date.

While Steve and Chris were investigating the deceased canine, another flock of birds was beginning to gather in San Clemente. It began when a field mouse had become the meal of a feral cat. The gray Tabby caught the rodent as it moved under the bleachers of the football field at the high school.

Typical of most cats, the mouser had made certain its prey was beyond escaping, but was now enjoying playing with his catch and had it in the middle of the field. A large gull came down and was now trying to steal the dead mouse from the cat. The cat was not amused and wondered if it shouldn't deal the same fate to this stupid bird as it gave the mouse.

While it was contemplating this, a second gull landed next to its companion. Then a crow came, and more curiously, a Mockingbird. After the fourth bird had encircled the hunter and its prey, the cat, confused and outnumbered, decided if they wanted the mouse that much they could have it.

Twenty minutes later the entire field was filled with hundreds of birds of various species. They had gathered on the bleachers, goal posts, and lighting stanchions as if this was the only place to roost in all of San Clemente. Birds that had never associated with other birds, of their species or not, were packed in with all the different types. Crows, gulls, pigeons, starlings, sparrows, vultures, even two owls were in the fray together. They had one common denominator Got to eat. Got to eat. GOTTA EAT!

A bell rang from the high school signaling that the extra curricular activity period had come to an end. Several students began to walk from the campus to awaiting cars and buses. The bell seemed to trigger something in the birds as well, and the vast gathering took wing at the sign of the first students coming out of the school.

They began a frenzied circling from the field and moved to the main campus. The flock was so large that several birds crashed head first into the buildings, which they could not see until too late. The thick cloud of birds caught up with the students moving away from the school. The teens couldn't see through the vast numbers of birds to their destination. They were pecked and jabbed as they tried to make it through the throng.

Several of the student body was on the ground trying to cover their face and other exposed parts of flesh from the impending onrush. Horns began honking, and people were getting out of cars and waving their arms and screaming at the top of their lungs at the chaos in front of them. Parents were panicked watching their children attacked by the birds.

Eventually, the birds began moving off, and any injured birds soon became prey instead of the predator. One particular dad was running through the parking lot kicking birds as hard as he could with pure unbridled rage as he ran for his daughter.

After about fifteen minutes the birds began to thin and disappear. The parents, faculty, and children stood in the parking lot with cuts and abrasions, but thankfully no critical injuries. A couple of the gashes were pretty big, but some bandages and antiseptic would tend to those wounds. Many of those who were in the attack looked to be in shock, or at least confused, about what had taken place and why.

The faculty moved through the injured to attend to their students. The less seriously hurt were sent home, while the more brutal attacks were taken to the nursing office of the school and treated further. The police were summoned through numerous frantic mobile phone calls, and when the first of three police cars arrived, they saw people meandering all over the parking lot with adults and children alike sitting or lying about the asphalt. There were dead birds scattered about them in various places around the buildings.

By the time the third police car made it to the campus, the officers had managed to gather most of the group together and were listening to wild tales of an attack by hundreds of birds of all types. The deputies just took notes and looked at each other with suspicious glances trying to figure out what happened to cause this mass hallucination. While the wounds were real, there had to be a more logical explanation than what they were hearing, dead birds included.

Only a couple birds could be seen winging their way

around the campus, and they did not seem particularly
vicious. All had seemingly returned to normal.

ᛕ ᛕᛏᛕ ᛕ ᛕᛏᛕ ᛕ ᛕᛏᛕ ᛕᛏ ᛕ ᛕᛏᛕ ᛕ ᛕᛏᛕ ᛕ ᛕᛏᛕ

Boomer had spent much of the day laying in his
field. He had begun to shun the daylight, as it hurt his
head so much. He also wasn't feeling like visiting people
anymore. He had decided he didn't like them or how
they called his name over and over.

After several days of eating everything in sight, he
was still hungry and thirsty. But now he didn't want to
eat, and he had become afraid of water. He never used
to be, but the mere sight of a bowl of water started him
growling. He felt like biting something, anything that
came past him.

His head hurt. It hurt badly. He wanted to be left
alone. He could hear the teenager approaching before he
could see him. Boomer had his eyes closed, wallowing in
pain. Jimmy Clow saw the dog laying by the sidewalk,
and as he always did, he greeted Boomer by saying,
"Hey Boomer, how's the best dog in San Clemente?"

Boomer did a low growl which caught Jimmy by
surprise. He had known Boomer for years and had never
known the dog to be anything but playful and loving.
He thought perhaps he found the dog in a bad dream.
So he reached down to give him his afternoon pets to
reassure him everything was all right.

He began scratching Boomer behind his ears as he
always did. The dog went ballistic and grabbed Jimmy

by the upper arm and bit down, hard.

Jimmy howled in pain and could see red leaking into his shirt underneath the dog's teeth. When Boomer finally released his grip, Jimmy pulled away and ran home screaming the entire way.

Boomer considered chasing after him and killing the boy.

When Jimmy got home, his mother dialed 911 and reported a feral dog attacked her son. She then called his father who said he would be home in a few moments and take him to the doctor.

Animal Control came to the house and went to the field reported by the boy. The officer found Boomer lying there with red and white foam in his mouth, growling at the approaching stranger. The man pulled his revolver, took aim, and fired.

He loaded the remains to take to the vet at Animal Control, but he already knew what they would find. He had seen rabid dogs before, and Boomer was one of those.

Poor kid, he is in for a lot more pain from rabies treatments, thought the officer.

The GPS on Chris' Dodge Charger led him up the hills that overlook the ocean to Surfside Drive where Tory was waiting by the front door when he pulled up. She came skipping down the front steps to his car in a light summer dress, and she looked completely different than she did in the khaki outfit she usually wore.

Chris was glad he wore his slacks and one of his better casual shirts. She reached the car and opened the door faster than Chris could get out of his side.

"Now how can I prove that I am a gentleman and have honorable intentions if you won't let me get your door?" he said in a deflated voice.

Tory laughed at his hurt look and said, "Okay, duly noted. I'm hungry, and I don't want to stand on ceremony. I'll give you a chance to redeem yourself after dinner. But for now, let's go eat."

He smiled and nodded and returned to the driver seat. "I'm glad you brought your appetite, I have a great place in mind." And he put the car in gear and pulled away from the curb.

Tory complimented him on his car and said she drove an old Jeep, which he had noticed in the driveway. He said that would make sense for field work, to which she laughed and said that's what she told everyone who saw it. She said she hoped to get something newer and sportier upon securing a permanent position.

They drove down the hill and returned to the main street of downtown San Clemente, Chris pulled into the back parking lot of Rosario's, and they walked around the front to the restaurant. Chris knew the owner of the bistro and asked the maitre d' if he was available. He learned there was an emergency and Angelo had to go home.

As the maitre d' took them to their table, Chris said he hoped it wasn't anything serious concerning Angelo or his family. The man replied he did not believe so, that apparently his son, along with some other students, had been attacked and injured by a flock of birds at the high school, and they were checking him out with their doctor. He seated them and left.

"Is this some joke?" asked an unamused Tory.

Chris was stunned by both comments, Tory's and the maitre d's and objected. "I had no idea about that. I hadn't heard anything about the high school," Chris said, "But if it is true then there must be something to all this. You're the expert, has anything like this ever happened? What about that old case you mentioned the other day?"

Tory bit her lip and looked squarely at Chris. "It was an isolated case, very violent and rapid," she said, "To this day, they never figured out what caused it or ended it."

"Tell me about it. Perhaps we can see similarities," pressed Chris.

"Not much to tell, really," she began, "It was in a town up the coast called Bodega Bay. For whatever reason, the birds went berserk and began attacking people. There were several deaths and a large number of injuries. It went on for a couple weeks. And then almost as suddenly as it began, the birds dropped dead, and nothing was ever found to explain it. The only unusual thing was that all the birds seemed bloated to the max. It was almost like they gorged themselves to death."

"That's what those gulls that attacked that young girl acted like. As if they were starving and couldn't get enough to eat," Chris said, "Maybe there is a connection?"

"Chris, that was nearly 60 years ago. Whatever happened back then couldn't possibly be related. No virus or disease can live that long in a vacuum. It would have to have been spread over the years somehow," Tory protested, "And there has never been another known situation like it."

Chris shrugged, "Yeah, until now." He spied the look Tory gave him and continued, "Well you must admit, there are some damn peculiar things going on around here that haven't happened before."

Chris related what happened while running with Steve and the dead dog. He said he had seen similar behavior on nature programs with the vultures in Africa and asked if there were any similarities?

She explained that there weren't that many vultures in one area around here, and that food was more plentiful because of the number of animals that fell victim to road kills and such.

"I beg to differ on the number of vultures you speak of," he said, "By my house, there is an entire flock that gathers in the high voltage towers. I see them every day."

"Even so, they would not normally swarm one dead dog like that. I actually can't imagine why the birds did," Tory answered Chris puzzled.

He finished by asking, "Do you think you should check out the high school?"

Tory began to think there was more to this than she

understood. "Perhaps I could make some inquiries, and then make a couple calls to my professor at UCSD. I don't know if he will have any more ideas than I do, but maybe he could talk to his colleagues and they would have a theory. I'll go to the high school tomorrow and see if they'll tell me anything."

"If you can't get anywhere let me know as I can talk to the cops and maybe get more information for you," finished Chris.

The waiter came up, and they ordered some wine and their dinners. They finally switched subjects and she talked about her aspirations and what got her started studying birds. "I always had a fascination with them ever since I could remember. My mother used to keep all types of bird feeders in Tennessee from seed and suet feeders to hummingbird feeders," she reminisced, "I used to watch them for what seemed like hours. I loved to hear their calls and see their colors."

"Tennessee, really?" asked Chris, "I thought I caught a little southern lilt in your speech."

"It's funny, nearly no one notices it now," she smiled as she spoke, "But put me back in Knoxville for a week and it becomes very pronounced all over again."

They spoke about how she came to California, his roots in The San Fernando Valley or just, "The Valley" as everyone in Southern California called it. He told her how he escaped to the beach after graduating college. They finished the bottle of wine while discussing their hopes and dreams for the future.

Chris felt pleased about how they were getting along

famously. He also decided that he genuinely liked Tory very much, and was not going to push this relationship along too fast and scare her off. After dinner they decided to walk up and down Avenida Del Mar and window shop before he drove her home. They talked more. She took his arm and and the couple strolled while the last of the fading light disappeared below the ocean.

When the date had ended, he played it cool and took her back to the house where she was staying. She gave him a brief kiss and walked back to the house, after saying she'd probably see him tomorrow.

As he came down the hill, he spotted the field lights at the high school football stadium. He decided on a little side trek toward it. From the football field, you could catch a glimpse of the ocean off in the distance. There was nothing untoward happening there now, though he spied a few dead birds laying close to the gymnasium next to the field. He recognized a crow, a sparrow, and a Mockingbird, and thought about how it was an unusual assortment.

He returned to his car and slowly pulled away from the school grounds. He hoped that the administration would be welcoming toward Tory and give her any help they could. Perhaps her being an expert would make them open up more than they usually would. He figured they would want answers as badly as he did.

He suddenly had a feeling of dread that he couldn't shake and wondered what was happening in this seaside resort.

Chapter 5 – Day 8

The morning was sparkling. Chris loved these days of late spring. They were so much better than when the haze of summer moved in. Then the days would be cloudy and hazy until mid-afternoon. These glorious mornings were clear, and Chris appreciated every one. The weatherman promised that it would be in the upper 70s again today and bright sunshine all day.

He retrieved his mail from yesterday and was looking around. He looked at the electric tower and what he saw surprised him. Turkey Vultures packed the top of the tower. There were many more than normal, he thought. As he could only see the very top, he moved to an area on the greenbelt where he could get a better view.

His stomach twisted as he could now see two-thirds of the tower and the wires leading to and from the structure. On all levels of the tower were dozens of vultures packed beak to tail feathers. When one vulture would open its wings or reposition itself, it almost knocked off others of its kind.

The wires leading up to and away from the tower were also crammed tight with crows, jays, mockingbirds, starlings, sparrows, pigeons and doves, and other birds of almost every type he had seen in California, except seabirds and hawks. There were no gulls, owls or hawks, but the sight was unbelievable. For most of the distance the birds perched on either side of the towers. If Chris guessed how many birds, he thought hundreds and possibly a thousand.

He ran into his house and grabbed his phone. He dashed out and took pictures of the sight he witnessed. He went back in and called Tory. When she answered, she said "My, you are a morning person aren't you? Miss me already?"

Chris completely missed Tory's playful mood, and said, "Tory, I just stepped out my door, and I saw something incredible. I am going to send you the pictures, and you can tell me if this is in any way normal."

Tory's tone changed instantly, and she said, "All right, send them, and I'll call you right back."

Chris hung up and did as Tory asked. Moments later his phone rang, and he answered. On the other end, Tory said, "May I assume this is going on right now and that this isn't in any way photo-shopped or pieced together?"

"This isn't any joke or ruse, I took the pictures and then I called you. Those pictures are as you see them," he answered.

"Chris, these birds don't flock together. And they would never sit between multiple species as these have done. This activity is extraordinary," she finished.

"It's worse than that, I couldn't get the full shot, and the lines are holding a lot more birds than I could fit into the frames," said a shaken Chris.

"I have a call in to a top ornithology professor I

know at Cornell University. She specializes in abnormal behavior in birds. I will also call my professor at UCSD later this morning. Until I hear back from them, I think I would stay clear of any gathering of birds, whether flying or perched," she said, "I plan to head over to the high school as soon as I am finished getting ready."

"Well I need to go to work, so I have no intention to see what might be in their bird brains this morning," said Chris, "I do worry about anyone who might stumble across this gaggle by mistake."

"Hopefully this is one of those strange innocent gatherings, and they all wound up on that wire together by accident," she said hesitantly.

"But you don't believe that, do you?" he said.

"No, not really," she admitted, "But until I get a reasonable explanation, I am not sure what I believe."

"Can we get together again this evening?" Chris asked, and then held his breath.

"Is this for academic reasons or more personal?" she taunted him.

"Well we can start academically if you wish, and then move toward more personal," he teased back to her.

"How about 6:30? I need to get some work done today, plus visiting the school," she said.

They agreed to meet at her house again and go from there. After Chris hung up, he grabbed a couple of cereal bars and ate them, then put on his lifeguard trunks and jacket. He grabbed his personal items and headed to the garage. As he backed the car out, he looked over to the tower. All the birds were gone, except a couple of vultures in a lower section.

Chris looked around and drove through the neighborhood to see if he could spot them roosting or circling somewhere. They couldn't be found anywhere. He didn't spot so much as a songbird, which was also unusual.

From his vantage point, he was unable to see the hollow on the other side of the greenbelt. There in the furrow were his missing birds and the poor old woman who had been attacked by them. At least what was left of her.

When Tory arrived at the high school, she went to the administration building to ask for the principal. When questioned as to what the visit concerned, she was greeted moments later by the dean of students.

Paul Arsenau was a big, stocky man who looked athletic in the build of a former football player. He had extremely close-cropped light brown hair. From a distance many guessed he was bald until they got closer to him. His eyes were small for his face, and they peered uncomfortably at anyone who looked back at him.

Tory was as pleasant as she could be, and offered to help with the bird incident at the high school yesterday.

Arsenau almost glared at her and said flatly, "Incident? What incident are you referring to?"

"I am a student of ornithology at UCSD, and I work

with the San Diego Zoological Society, and I understand your students had an altercation with birds yesterday," she said quickly.

"Oh, I wouldn't call it an altercation," said Arsenau and he narrowed his eyes further, "It was a flock of birds that became misdirected and flew into a group of students."

Tory's eyes widened in disbelief, and she said, "So there was no one injured, and the birds did not show any aggression?"

Arsenau tried to act more pleasantly and said, "Oh, well, there may have been a few scratches when the birds accidentally flew into a couple students. But the poor things were obviously confused and were trying to get their bearings again. They flew off once they did. We were able to get the students attended to afterward. Nothing serious, I assure you."

"I understand the police were called in? Was that their assessment as well?" she asked pointedly.

"Are you a student or a reporter?" questioned Arsenau, any trace of his of his humor now gone, "The police come to the school at ANY unusual occurrence on campus. It is a matter of routine to guarantee the safety of our students. Now if you will excuse me, I have other duties to attend to."

Tory decided to try a different tact, "Is there anyone available I can talk to who witnessed the event? I am working on a thesis concerning the migration and mating habits of coastal birds, and this may figure into my paper."

Arsenau said, "Miss, I am not even sure which students were on campus at the time. Plus they are all in classes currently, and I cannot dismiss them for this line of questioning from you."

"Line of questioning?" Tory was irritated at this bureaucrat's stonewalling and deception, "Look, I am just trying to offer assistance and any help I can to try and explain or discover what might have happened. I'll figure this out later, and when the press does come around to ask me the cause of all this, I will make certain to comment how helpful and concerned you were in helping me find out what hurt your students!"

She spun on her heels and started to storm off.

Arsenau gave a smug look and turned the opposite direction. As he walked off, he muttered under his breath, "Students. No matter how long they are out of high school they are still a pain in the ass."

When Tory relayed the conversation she had at the high school, Chris said he would see what he could find out. He called his friends at the sheriff's office, but because the deputies in question had arrived at the scene after the incident was over, they couldn't offer any help, and their report was sketchy at best.

It said that an undetermined number of birds had swarmed the high school and had tangled up with a group of students leaving after the extra period expired. Some of the students received minor cuts and abrasions, but there were no life-threatening injuries, and all the students treated and released to the custody of their parents, end of story.

Later in the day, Professor Ellen Revere from Cornell University returned Tory's call. The last thing Tory wanted to sound like was an alarmist to this noted ornithologist. She did her best to explain some of the goings on around San Clemente, without putting too much emotion into it.

There was a measured silence, and then Prof. Revere said, "Well dear, it sounds like you have stumbled into some very unusual traits with the birds out there. I don't quite know what to say, or how to respond to the behaviors you are witnessing."

"So you don't believe me, then," said Tory, deflated.

"No dear, I believe you, I don't have any theories on what is causing this strange behavior. You say they seem to be exhibiting carnivorous tendencies? I just have never known birds, beyond the usual birds of prey, to exhibit such habits." the professor explained.

Tory didn't know how to continue this discussion without sounding like a lunatic. She said, "I thought it was extremely ridiculous myself at first, but I must admit, something seems to be affecting these birds."

"Do you have any of the birds involved in these attacks, living or dead?" asked Prof. Revere.

"No, not yet," answered Tory.

"I'll tell you what, if you capture one and send it to our lab here at Cornell, we will run a series of tests to see if there is something physiological about what might be causing this behavior," the ornithologist said, "Until then, I can't help you much. I am curious about these situations. You know, I was a high school student when the Bodega Bay incident happened. Years later, I wished I had the chance to do field research on that event."

Tory couldn't help herself and replied, "Be careful what you wish for, you may get it."

The professor on the other end of the phone laughed and said, "Well, if your town's incident turns out to be half that interesting, I'll take the first plane out!"

"Promise?" said Tory immediately, "If I can't figure this out with the help of my colleagues and professors at UCSD, I'm calling you."

"Okay, that's a deal," said Prof. Revere, "Keep my number handy and get me a specimen to examine. I will keep an eye out on the Internet for any stories in Southern California, or elsewhere, about other such reports and keep you apprised of any similarities."

"Thank you, Prof. Revere, I would appreciate it," said Tory.

"You're welcome Tory, I'll be in touch," and with that, she was gone.

When Chris and she got together later, Tory discussed her conversation with Prof. Revere. "At least she didn't think I was some fruitcake."

"Just because you are giving her some unusual behavioral habits of the birds down here shouldn't make anyone think you are a 'fruitcake'," Chris said, "After all, even she brought up Bodega Bay. I didn't know about that story."

"That's what a lot of leaders in the field call it – a story," recounted Tory, "Many of them insist that it is a fairy tale, or urban legend, and didn't happen. At least not explainable to them."

"There are always naysayers on any event," said Chris, "It's almost as if their acceptance is needed to round out the story and make it believable. Hey, you said that Prof. Revere wanted samples? Perhaps there are a couple of dead birds left at the school?"

"We can go back there after dinner, I know I saw a few scattered around as I went into the building," said Tory excitedly.

"I don't know why I didn't think to stop and examine them," she added. "I guess I was so rattled when I came out, I didn't give it a thought. That guy Arsenau is quite a piece of work. I got the impression that he wouldn't have cared if the birds had carried off a student or two," she said in disgust.

"I'm sure he was protecting his position at the school," said Chris, "After all, I never understood what a dean of students did exactly. I thought for a while it was the same as a Truant Officer, but I am not sure. But yeah, we will go over and get a couple of birds and get them off to Cornell and UCSD."

Tory was still focused on Arsenau and said, "That's what he looked like to me, one of those bullies we grew up with that got recycled in an education program because he wasn't able to do anything else." Tory was venting poison now.

"Well let's forget about him," Chris said anxiously to improve her mood, "What would my lady like to do this evening in my town?"

"Oh, your town is it?" she laughed. Then she thought for a moment, "After the high school, how about taking me to that beach where they found that boy?"

"Um...I think they still have it closed off, and heading over to a murder scene doesn't sound like too much fun to me," Chris said. He was hoping for something a little more romantic than surveying scenes of mayhem and death.

"Oh, and now it's a murder scene?" Tory asked. Chris just shrugged his shoulders. "Call it a burning curiosity. If it is still roped off, then we won't interfere, I want to see if I can figure anything out. Plus I need more information for Prof. Revere," she argued.

"Well never let it be said that Chris Palmer didn't know how to show a girl a good time!" he boasted, "Even though he might get arrested doing it. Okay, we'll go."

They first went over to the school. Chris didn't mention to Tory that he had gone by last night but knew where he had spotted several of the birds from the attack. When they got there, they combed the grounds but couldn't find any birds remaining.

"That's strange," said Tory, "I could have sworn there were several dead birds around here."

"Maybe the janitors picked them up and got rid of them," said Chris, "I am sure the administration didn't want them stinking up the place."

They found the outside dumpsters and looked inside but found nothing except discarded papers. After some more time, they gave up and got back in Chris' car.

When they got to the beach, Chris was surprised to see that there was no barrier and nothing to prevent them from walking to where the sheriff's deputies found the young man. In fact, there was nothing to show that the incident had ever happened. The couple walked from the parking lot over to the place that Chris surmised must have been the scene of the crime.

The sand had been raked clean. There was no sign of the tape or rebar erected previously. Chris scratched his head and said, "Well this is very strange."

"Maybe this is the wrong beach?' Tory asked.

"No, it's the right beach. This is the one the sheriff's deputies said in the report I heard. But not a sign of what might have happened. Almost like it was erased," Chris said

CHAPTER 6 – DAY 10

A couple of days later, Andy did not feel at all well. It had begun the previous day with an elevated temperature and a sore throat. This morning he could tell he was running a full-on fever and had a violent headache. He moved out of his hidey hole, as he called it, but couldn't move too quickly and seemed weak and disoriented. His side where attacked felt tingly. When he touched it, it was painful, and he saw it was inflamed. The sun hurt his eyes and head.

As he began to come away from the grassy area he stayed at during the night he became confused and wobbly. He was angry about his condition and knew it was Birdzilla that was the cause. With great effort, he finally made it down to the beach and over to Steve's station.

Steve looked down at Andy and had just asked him how he was doing. He watched Andy collapse in a pile at the base of the elevated chair. Steve jumped down and began checking Andy out. Steve could tell he was burning up and said he would get him some water.

"No damn water, I don't want to see a glass of anything," said Andy with a harsh voice, "If you bring me any water, I'll kill you!" He then passed out at Steve's feet.

Steve radioed for an ambulance. By the time they

arrived, Andy was unresponsive to treatment and remained unconscious. They had loaded him into the ambulance and took him to the nearest hospital. When Andy arrived at the emergency entrance, they determined he was in a coma.

Information on Andy was little and would remain that way. Two hours later Andy died. They attributed it to exposure, complicated by the flu. After all, he was homeless for years and in his sixties. It was bound to happen eventually.

On that same morning, Rachel Tillinghast also checked into a hospital near her home in Santa Ana. Her mother had taken her to their doctor the day before when her daughter complained of a sore throat and difficulty swallowing. When her mother tried to bring Rachel some juice, she slapped it away from her mother and told her she wanted nothing to drink.

Rachel had never shown an aggressive moment to her mother in her life. This more than any other symptom scared her mother into action. Rachel was also suffering from a fever, headache, and general weakness through her body. At the doctor's office, she had a temperature of 101 degrees. The doctor said Rachel must have picked up a flu bug and prescribed antibiotics to treat the problem. He said if she became worse to get her back in and they would run tests.

That morning, Rachel collapsed in the kitchen and banged her head against the counter badly enough to make it bleed. Her mother covered the wound with a wet cloth and ran her to the emergency room. Rachel wasn't responding to treatment, and they said her temperature was now 102.5 and that she had lost consciousness and was unable to be revived. She lay in bed with her parents around her, in a comatose state. The doctors determined that she had hit her head sufficiently hard enough to cause the coma. They thought the fall could also cause brain damage, along with the flu virus based on her doctor's prognosis the day before.

Their only treatment was to keep fluids and antibiotics coursing through her, and hoped she would recover from her fall.

It would not be enough.

$$\kappa \, \iota^{\iota} \kappa \quad \kappa \, \iota^{\iota} \kappa \, \iota^{\iota} \kappa \, \iota^{\iota} \kappa \quad \kappa \, \iota^{\iota} \kappa \, \iota^{\iota} \kappa \quad \kappa \, \iota^{\iota} \kappa$$

Captain Ben Riley finished preparing his boat the Flying Fin and was expecting his charters at any moment. He listened to the reports that morning and learned that there was a good bite on around North Beach at San Clemente past the shoal. The captain heard they were hooking Giant White Sea Bass more than 30 pounds yesterday and today seemed good as well. He had loaded the bait, the refreshments stowed, and his mate was checking the rods and lines. It promised to be a great day with clear skies and calm waves.

He heard them even before he saw the young couple coming down the pier. When he looked up, he could see they were all smiles and playfully teasing each other.

Ben thought he wouldn't be disappointed looking at those long legs that ended in very short shorts on the young lady all day long. He hoped that a bikini top was under the windbreaker that might be revealed later in the day when it warmed.

He met them when they reached the boat and welcomed them aboard. The young man had told Ben that he had always wanted to go deep sea fishing and that his fiance got him this trip for his birthday. Ben promised the young man, whose name was John, that he would have a perfect birthday and would land some good fish today. His girlfriend Kathy wasn't interested in fishing but loved being out on a boat. She told the captain, the fishing was for John, that she just hoped to soak up some sun and work on her tan later.

To Capt. Ben, this day was already sounding more promising.

He told his mate, Mario, to cast the lines off and that it was time to get going. He carefully backed his boat out of its slip at Dana Point and upon clearing the breakwaters headed south.

ᴋ ᴋᵗᴋ ᴋ ᴋᵗᴋᵗ ᴋ ᴋᵗᴋᵗ ᴋ ᴋᵗ ᴋ ᴋᵗᴋᵗ ᴋ ᴋᵗ ᴋ ᴋ ᴋᵗ ᴋ

Got to eat. Got to eat. GOTTA EAT! It was all that was on the minds of the gulls that were flying around the coast near North Beach. They had been fishing and had found a small school of fish, but they lost it almost as quickly as they saw it. Earlier they would find a mouse or crab near the shore, but it wasn't enough, and every gull was fighting for each morsel.

And worse, there seemed to be more and more competition for everything. The gulls were coming from everywhere. They would circle tighter and tighter looking for any thing they could get in their beaks.

Many of the birds had been around some of the fishing boats farther out at sea, but it seemed to take too much effort to fly that far west to grab slim pickings, as a handful of birds could be easily fought off. They kept circling the shoal by North Beach in hopes of finding something more appetizing, but they were starving in their search.

Before too long they were snapping at each other during their aerial maneuvers. They had become desperate in their search for food and angry. A lone pigeon had flown into the flock and was immediately taken down. Several birds sat on the water picking at the misguided bird that was now ripped asunder and bobbing on the water like a cork.

The remainder of the birds still were circling hoping to find another school of fish to charge. Their displays and shrieks attracted more gulls from either side of the coast. Before too long there were hundreds of birds gathering again, mostly in the air, but a full congregation was riding the waves as well.

The Flying Fin was staying closer to the shore as Capt. Ben had been following a pod of dolphins to the delight of Kathy and John. Capt. Ben figured he could break west when they got closer to their destination. It was always important to give the customers as much fun as possible, regardless if it involved intense fishing or playing with dolphins, seals or whales.

They came around the bend and Capt. Ben saw the massive number of birds. He had seen gulls gather up like this before. Capt. Ben wrongly guessed that there must be a school of fish in the center of the flock. Instead of taking corrective measures to move away from the congregation, he headed straight at them.

As he approached, he couldn't believe his luck, as there were so many birds that this must be a tremendous ball of bait fish which was bound to attract bigger fish, possibly even tuna, including bluefin and yellowtail. He had never seen this many birds all packed together in the air and on the waves, and had yelled over the engine to his passengers that they were in for the time of their lives.

The birds that were on the waves took wing and knew that their luck had just changed, too. They began circling in a tight ball again and were soon all over the Flying Fin and its crew. This time they weren't after just bait but started attacking the passengers. Capt. Ben was swinging his arms around and hitting several of the winged attackers. But for each one he struck, he was attacked by a half dozen more.

They were all over the deck biting at legs, feet, and anything they could. Kathy was screaming as loud as she could, but the birds screeched louder and drowned out her pleas for help. John had tripped over one of the coolers and was now spread out on the deck and covered in birds.

All the while more and more birds joined the bombardment. From a short distance away one would not know there was a boat, only birds frantically winging around in a tight circle.

They stabbed and tore at every inch of exposed flesh. Blood was now staining the deck red. Capt. Ben had birds all over his head and face and lost his footing. He fell to the deck below.

Mario had come out of the hold to help his captain and passengers and was overcome by the birds. He fought as hard as he could and then decided that he was safer in the water and dove overboard into the ocean. They were a good three hundred yards from the shore, and as he came up for breath, the birds would overtake him making it impossible to get more than a gulp of air into his lungs.

Many of the gulls aimed for the softer spots on his face such as eyes, ears, and cheeks and soon he was blinded in one eye, and he had gashes all over his face, while alternately trying to breathe and scream at the same time.

The pool of blood began overflowing from the deck into the ocean. As the blood reached the water, it attracted a whole new predator. In an unusual sight for Southern California, there were now several sharks patrolling around the boat.

Mario felt something hit his leg and knew it wasn't a bird. Moments later he felt a burning sensation on his calf and knew that his problems had just increased. He tried splashing and yelling but it was to no avail. Mario got hit again, and this time by a much more prominent fish. It took his leg off and severed the femoral artery. He was still gasping for air and took one last gulp as he felt himself fade from consciousness. As he began to sink into the deeper water, he wondered if he'd drown or bleed out first, being attacked from above and below the water.

Mario's fate was decided a moment later when several sharks began attacking in waves. A great white delivered the final fatal blow, while another shark ripped his arm from its socket.

Capt. Ben had lost his sight as both his eyes had been pecked out and he couldn't see to protect himself. He tried standing up several times but the constant attack by the birds and the damage they had inflicted proved too much for him. The entire ship was invisible and covered in gulls. A massive bevy of birds still encircled the craft from above.

Just before losing his sight he saw Kathy facing upwards and her body riddled with cuts and nearly shredded in some places. The birds had broken through the windbreaker, but there was so much blood that Capt. Ben never did see what she was wearing underneath it. He knew that she was dead as the birds were pecking at the lifeless body with no reaction from her.

Similarly, John was laying at the stern rolled up like a ball. Capt. Ben could not see his face but knew if he were alive, it would not be for long. Like Kathy, John was covered entirely in blood-soaked birds who continued their decimation of his body with no reprisals from John.

Inside of 30 minutes a birthday fishing trip turned into a scene of horrifying carnage. An hour after the boat sailed into the storm, the birds had moved on from the ship, and it eerily bobbed at a slow pace with the engine rumbling forward toward the shore. It would be found a couple of hours later when it ran aground a half-mile from the San Clemente Pier.

Tory had to finish reports that were past due on her migrating and nesting waterfowl. She was already under the gun to cram as much data as she could into her statement. She found that the time spent investigating the other bird problem in San Clemente had put her seriously behind.

She was watching a larger than typical flock of pelicans cruising a hair's breath above the waves. There were two males and a band of females in tow. Tory watched mystified as to how they could fly so close to the water and not crash into it, or even dampen a wing. As she was making notes about their movement, she looked up and saw a gull come out of nowhere and flew into one of the females knocking her into the water.

The remaining pelicans continued without breaking formation. The female pelican attempted to regain its ascent to the sky, but the gull continued its pursuit. Then a second and third gull joined in on the raid. Soon six or seven gulls were attacking the pelican like a swarm of ants on a bug.

Eventually, the pelican was defeated, and Tory witnessed the gulls rip the bird apart. She tried to take a couple of pictures with her phone, but she was too far away, and between the waves and the continuous movement made it impossible for anything to be seen.

She had not witnessed or even heard of such behavior from birds other than certain hawks. And certainly not on another larger bird. She knew how crows and mockingbirds would stave off other birds of prey from their nest, but this was an entirely different situation.

Being omnivorous, gulls were known to eat nearly anything they could grab. But again, there hadn't been reports of them attacking seemingly healthy birds. Tory closed her notebook and moved to a bench by the area where the grass stopped, and the sand started.

She grabbed her phone again and made a call. After four rings a voice came on and said, "Forrester."

"Dr. Forrester, this is Tory McKnight," she said.

"Tory! Well, I was beginning to think that you were carried off by merpeople in San Clemente, how are you?" Forrester joked with her.

"I'm fine, but I think we might have a problem with the aviary population in San Clemente," she said without a trace of humor in return.

"Okay, what's happening?" asked Dr. Forrester.

Dr. Bill Forrester was her favorite professor at UCSD, and he was arguably the most prominent reason she had gone into aviary science so passionately. He had studied birds all over the globe, including such exotic places like Galapagos and Antarctica. He was about 50 years old and had rugged, handsome features. Listening to him discussing the anatomy, movement and behavior of birds seemed almost as fluid as the birds themselves.

Tory spent the next fifteen minutes explaining what had been taking place in San Clemente to a mostly silent professor on the other end.

When she finished, Forrester said, "You realize Tory, that you are describing behaviors that have not been witnessed before and would have most experts dismiss this as so much bunk."

"If I hadn't just seen this event followed on the heels of two other incidents, I would be saying the same," she said in a matter-of-fact tone.

"I see," Forrester paused, "Well then I think I may have to take a ride up there and see this for myself."

Tory made a fist and pushed it triumphantly through the air. Yes! She thought silently. She asked how soon she could expect him.

"I have a few things to take care of here. I can get one of my teaching assistants to take over my summer classes. I can leave this afternoon, or tomorrow morning at the latest," Forrester responded, "You know Tory if it was anyone but you, I don't know that I would put much stock in this. But you are one of my best students, and I am curious to see this behavior myself."

"I appreciate this so much, Dr. Forrester," said a relieved Tory, "I have no idea what might be causing this, but if it is true, we could be looking at another

Bodega Bay."

"Let's not jump to any conclusions like that one, shall we?" said the professor, "That incident was never solved, and I suspect it is a more urban legend than fact by now."

"Yes, sir," answered Tory.

"I'll see you soon Tory," replied Dr. Forrester. "I'll call this number when I get into town." He said goodbye and was gone. Tory then called Chris to let him know.

Mayor Jean Turkovitch was a witch, pure and simple. She was such an evil character that she stunted the growth of her children by feeding them massive doses of behavioral drugs. All so she wouldn't have to cope with their personalities.

How she became the leader of San Clemente had nothing to do with her experience, knowledge or personality. Her father, David Irvin became a big deal in the produce supply game and amassed a substantial amount of wealth. He would rub shoulders with political kingpins including former President Richard Nixon at the Western White House, as it was known. In addition to money, he also had a substantial supply of political and economic favors that he banked away for a rainy day.

So when his daughter decided she wanted to be important, daddy bought her an appointment to the city council. He knew his daughter wouldn't be able to accomplish much in her false way of dealing with people. He also knew looks wouldn't work. His daughter had severe acne problems while growing up, and no amount of makeup could cover the moon surface scarring she had on her face.

As his daughter's insatiable appetite grew for more power and control, he got her elected as mayor and through favors, kept her there. It was as much as she would attain, as even he did not have enough clout or money to get her any higher in the California political system. And now she sat looking out over her office in her home by the shore, and she was fuming.

Goddam birds, she thought, *What the hell is going on? This close to tourist season and this close to the Microbrew Fest. That always kicks off our busiest season.* It was her feathers that were ruffled, and she didn't like it one bit.

It had been Turkovitch that was the driving force behind stifling the rumors and stories about the attacks. She was unconcerned for the students, and even the tourists didn't affect her unless they decided not to show up. No, she only worried about whether the economy would do as well as previous years or better. Nothing else mattered.

The beautification project, the new mall, the beach revitalization, and cleanups all meant one thing to Turkovitch. Money, and lots of it pouring into San Clemente that would assure her position in the community. Plus a little kickback now and then didn't hurt her personal financial situation either. And now, of all the damnedest things that might jeopardize it, birds.

What Chris and Tory and most others were unaware of was that birds had been attacking pedestrians all over San Clemente and the neighboring towns of San Juan Capistrano, Dana Point, and Capistrano Beach for the last several days. She had been in touch with the other leaders of those towns and had told them in no uncertain terms to keep a lid on things, as she was doing in her neighborhood.

Most of the attacks weren't dangerous and were over as quickly as they started. Many involved a quick swoop, peck and then off again. Turkovitch had never known of such attacks and really couldn't give a shit as to what caused it or why. She was more concerned about it scaring off the tourists.

Damn tourists are so fickle about every stupid thing already, she thought, looking at a flock of gulls flying outside her window. *I already have enough to deal with; rain, temperatures, the nation's economy, whether it is a bad cold or flu season. And now goddam birds.*

Well, this year was going to be the town's best and so help her, no damn birds were going to put a fly in that ointment. She got up and went to finish getting ready for the Chamber of Commerce meeting she was due to be at that morning. She was about to make sure that they didn't panic. They'd better keep quiet just like her, or heaven help them.

ᴋᴋᵗᴋ ᴋᴋᵗᴋᴋᴋᵗᴋᴋ ᵗᴋ ᴋᴋᵗᴋᴋᴋᵗᴋ ᴋᴋᵗᴋ

Later that day, Lt. Joe Ferguson had come away from

the examination room of the morgue still shaking his head. He had taken numerous forensic courses and had examined the remains twice already with the pathologist at the coroner's office. He rubbed his mostly bald head and stood to his full six foot three stature. He carried a bit of a belly, but at 59 was in pretty good shape and could run down a perpetrator if the need arose. At least so long as it was a short sprint.

The parents of the victim were demanding the release of their son's remains, as it had been a couple of days now, and neither he nor the doctor had any promising idea of what caused the death of the young man.

They knew there was a high alcohol content in his blood, drugs would not appear for a couple more days, but neither of these looked to have anything to do with his demise.

"Massive blood loss" was all the doctor put on the report. When Ferguson looked at it, he just squinted sideways at the doctor and said, "Yeah, no shit. You think?"

Doctor James Bennett just shrugged and said, "I still can't find any entry wounds or damage from a gun or knife. No trauma to the head or bruising anywhere. And while he looks like he went through a meat processing plant, there are no bite marks or broken bones. I'm stumped."

"What about the bird angle?" asked the lieutenant, "I am hearing some strange stories around town the last couple days."

The doctor laughed and said, "Unless we have a Pterodactyl that moved into the area, I just can't imagine a bird, or a whole damn flock, doing this kind of carnage. Plus most birds aren't carnivorous beyond eating a few bugs."

Lt. Ferguson nodded his head and finally gave up himself. He turned and moved out of the morgue. The parents were pushing his department for answers, and he had none to give, not even an apparent cause of death.

The mayor had insisted in taking down the barriers to the scene the next day and even sent a maintenance crew out to rake out the sand and clean it up, so there was no purpose in going back there for answers. Damn politicians are always getting in the way of his job.

He questioned the first officers on the scene again, but neither had shed any more light on this since the first report. He was about to head back to his office when a call came over his radio for him to hustle out to the beach area. A boat had just washed ashore with three corpses on it.

Lt. Ferguson thought this was going to be a helluva month.

He got into his car and drove down to North Beach. As he pulled into the parking area, he spotted two other Sheriff's deputy cars with their lights flashing and pulled alongside. He got out and saw the officers down the beach about a hundred yards with two standing on the sand and two on the boat. The craft was listing about 30 degrees to starboard, and he could see the officers were having trouble holding their ground.

When he got to the boat, he got a hand up from one of his other deputies. Deputy Jim Schultz was a strong black man with the best humor on the force. But he wasn't in a good mood today. He looked at Lt. Ferguson and said, "Christ Chief three of them just carved up like steaks. I had never heard of pirates around the south coast, but I gotta. believe that is what caused this."

"Do we know where they're from?" asked Ferguson.

"Yeah, we radioed it in, it's a charter boat out of Dana Point. They came out this morning, supposedly to do a little fishing. My guess is it was a drug deal that went south," said Dep. Schultz.

"Why not just kill them?" asked the lieutenant. "Why the big mess?"

"Makes a statement," answered Dep. Schultz, "Says 'don't fuck with us' or else this will be you."

It wasn't a terrible theory, thought Ferguson. But it didn't feel right. "Anything else on the boat?" asked the lieutenant, "Guns, liquor, drugs, cash?"

"Nothing, except two cases of beer and a flare gun," said Schultz.

"How tore up is the cabin?" asked Ferguson.

"Untouched, they must have found what they wanted topside," answered the deputy.

"So you think pirates came aboard, seized whatever they were after, chopped three people up and didn't bother to check the rest of the boat for anything else?" said the lieutenant, "That makes no sense to me. Were the victims shot?"

"Not that Jake or I saw, just butchered. Almost like they were tortured." Dep. Schultz said, disgustedly.

Then Ferguson saw it again. Bird tracks all over the deck. Especially several tracks up by where he knew his officers couldn't have walked because of the angle of the boat. "What's that?" asked the senior officer.

"Apparently some seagulls must have landed on the boat while it was drifting." said Schultz, "They tracked the blood all over the deck. There was so much blood I couldn't tell at first myself."

Then Deputy Jake Randall came out of the cabin area, "Hell of a mess, hey Cap? They sure must of pissed somebody off."

Lt. Ferguson looked at both men and calmly said, "I don't think so. I think you may both be mistaken. For one thing, if they were carved up like this, where are the pieces?"

"Thrown over the side for the fish," answered Dep. Randall.

"Why? Why would you make a statement like this and not leave the remains?" asked Lt. Ferguson, "And why isn't the boat torn apart? If someone went to all the trouble of filleting these bodies to make a point, why wouldn't they tear up the rest of the boat looking for anything they could find? And lastly, why are there bird tracks all over the deck, but no shoe or footprints? How could the birds track everything, but anyone else not leave one footprint?"

"Okay, not pirates, then what?" asked Dep. Schultz.

"Look at the damage to their faces, eyes plucked out,

flesh ripped off exposed areas, interior organ damage, but no bullet holes or shells laying around, possible knife cuts, but doesn't look the same. I just left a body like this in the morgue."

"You mean the kid on the beach from the other day?" asked Dep. Randall, "Do you think they are related? Do we have a crazed serial killer?"

"No," said the lieutenant as he examined Capt. Ben's remains, "I think we have a bigger problem, and I am not sure what to do about it."

Deputies Schultz and Randall looked at their lieutenant and wondered what he could be saying. But then again, neither of them had seen anything like this in their sleepy seaside town before. Four bodies in a week were big news, even though they were under strict orders not to talk about the first one.

Lt. Ferguson ordered the area sealed off, and this time he wasn't going to let Turkovitch take it down until he was satisfied. Even if he had to go to the governor to see to it. He watched as the bodies were loaded into the wagon and wondered just what the hell was going on around here.

He was watching a gull walk around the beach, but it sure didn't seem to be acting at all peculiar. As he stepped toward it, it flew off and out of sight. He punched up the doctor on his phone and told him about the three new victims and said he wanted to meet him there as soon as they came in to look at all four victims together for similarities.

Lt. Ferguson was aware of the incident at the high

school but hadn't given it any thought until now. Pieces were beginning to come together, and he didn't like the picture it was forming. He radioed to the station and asked them to put a copy of the high school report and anything else that might have happened in the last couple weeks that involved birds.

"Check with the fire department, hospital and lifeguard stations as well," he said, "I want anything that even mentions the word 'bird' in it. And I need it fast, I'll be at the morgue, but then I'm heading back when I finish."

Lt. Ferguson knew there was no need to run with lights on as there would be no sense to beat the wagons to the morgue. He decided to get a cup of coffee and went through the drive-through at the local Starbucks. As he sat waiting for his cup of brew, he watched an old man sauntering across the street.

He saw a crow come off a ledge of the building and strike the old man on his shoulder and fly off. The old man was surprised but unhurt. He cursed the crow and kept walking.

Ferguson thought to himself, *What the hell is going on around here?*

When he made it back to the morgue, he met Dr. Bennett again. Bennett was a thin man in his sixties with just a few wisps of hair that he plastered to the top of his head. He wore glasses for close work. Otherwise, Bennett kept them on the top of his head. He had them in place now as he bent over the first of the three victims just brought in.

"Interesting," the doctor commented, "The lacerations and internal injuries look to be the same as our student over there."

"Ideas on a cause of death now?" asked Lt. Ferguson, "That is, besides massive blood loss?"

The doctor looked up at the lieutenant and lifted his glasses. "What is it you believe did this? Because you ask like you are waiting for a confirmation," he said suspiciously.

"I am," Lt. Ferguson said unflinching, "Give me your best shot, no matter how absurd you may think it sounds."

The doctor went to the second corpse and looked carefully at the tissue damage. As he did this, he said more to himself, "Flesh looks torn, not cut. There existed several gashes in proximity to each wound. Tremendous damage from smooth, not serrated incisions. Soft tissue areas have the most deterioration and lacerations. Multiple depths and sizes of cuts."

When the doctor finished examining the young girl, he stood up and arched his back.

"Well?" asked Lt. Ferguson.

"Joe, I will tell you, but if you put this into a report I may deny I said it," Dr. Bennett said, "It looks like beak marks throughout the whole body. I can't be positive if that is what caused the death, but it is what caused all the trauma following if it is not the original cause."

"Beak marks, like from birds?" asked the lieutenant.

"I know it sounds crazy, but again, I see no bruising

or entry wounds from any other source that I can determine. No bullet, knife, or needle marks, nothing. And I'll bet these three won't have any alcohol or other substance that shows up in the prelim test," finished the doctor.

"How many birds would it take to cause this amount of devastation?" asked Lt. Ferguson.

"Hard to guess without knowing what kind of birds, or how long it took," said the doctor.

"Let's say seagulls and not much time," interjected Lt. Ferguson.

"Seagulls? Damn, to take on all three it would have to be 50 or more birds. In fact, assuming that some would have given up or retreated, I'd guess more like a hundred for all three victims at the same time." said Dr. Bennett.

Lt. Ferguson stood looking at what was left of the girl and tried to imagine her horror at a vicious swarm of birds eating her alive.

"Did you see any birds on the boat while there?" asked Dr. Bennett.

Lt. Ferguson shook his head, "No, not physically, just a whole mass of bloody tracks around the boat."

"You do know what we are talking about is nothing short of science fiction, or a bad horror flick at the least?" the doctor protested.

"As Sherlock Holmes said, 'When you have eliminated the impossible, whatever remains, however improbable, must be the truth,'" said Lt. Ferguson.

"Yeah but, birds?" asked Dr. Bennett, "What could

make them go into that kind of a frenzy?"

"I have no idea, but if bees and ants can kill people, why not birds?" reasoned Lt. Ferguson, "And there was an attack at the high school by birds the other day. As mysterious as this, but without the fatalities."

"Yeah but Joe, ants and bees don't consume their victims afterward," said Dr. Bennett.

Lt. Ferguson just shrugged. He wasn't sure what the answer to that was, but he now suspected he had the culprit or culprits responsible for the massacre. The lieutenant just needed to verify it at his office. He said, "When you finish examining the third victim, I expect to see a cause on that report, and it will say bird attack. Unless you can come up with a more plausible explanation, and I want an immediate call if you do."

Lt. Ferguson turned and left the doctor to his examinations. As the lieutenant headed for his car to get to the station, Dr. James Bennett pulled out his phone and called up his contact list as quickly as possible.

"And one last thing, I expect the biggest crowd we have ever had at this festival no matter what it takes to get them there," Turkovitch was saying to the Chamber of Commerce Executive Committee, "Whatever advertising or efforts it takes. Last year's turnout was dismal compared to the predictions. So we ALL need to do a better job on this year's events."

Her phone began ringing, and she hit the machine

saying, "I am in a meeting, so this better be damn important."

As Turkovitch listened her brow furrowed and then her eyes got bigger, she finally spoke into the phone with poison in her voice, "You better NOT put that in the goddamn report. I don't care what he said. What are you trying to do? Cause a panic? It must have been some accident, and the boat somehow chewed them up. Listen I don't care what happened; you don't dare put anything in there that would adversely affect our town or I'll have your license for it." She hit the phone again and wheeled on the Chamber committee.

"Problem?" asked the executive director.

"Nothing, any of you, need to be concerned with," she said harshly, "Just keep your focus on the festival next week and how we can bring more people out to the beach this season. If one more person tells me about how crappy the economy is in Southern California and that is why we are having fiscal problems, that person will find themselves stranded on San Clemente Island!"

After the meeting, Turkovitch left the Chamber office and headed back to her own. As soon as she entered the office, she closed the door and dialed the Orange County Sheriff's Office. When they picked up, she barked, "Under-sheriff Puerta, it's urgent."

She didn't have to identify herself as they all knew Turkovitch when she called. A moment later the phone connected and she heard, "Jose Puerta."

"Listen, Puerta, this is the second time I have had to call you about an incident involving Ferguson within a week. If you expect support from our communities to get that Sheriff position that you are in line for, you better put a leash on your dog and rein him in."

"Madame Mayor, I assure you Lt. Ferguson is trying to keep your community safe, and right now you have four unexplained deaths," Puerta tried to reason with her.

"Listen, I do not care what he 'thinks' he is doing. If he creates an incident around here that scares off our commerce, then I will have the governor intervene, and you will be back to writing traffic tickets within a month, do I make myself clear?"

Turkovitch spat all that in one fluid sentence then slammed the phone down. *Damn Sheriff's Office think they can do what they want in my town; I'll chew them up and spit them out before they know what hit them.*

ᏦᏦᏦ ᏦᏦᏦ ᏦᏦᏦ ᏦᏦ ᏦᏦᏦᏦ ᏦᏦᏦᏦ ᏦᏦᏦ

Lt. Ferguson arrived at his office, and there was a stack of reports waiting for him when he got there. He flipped through several of them. There were numerous reports over the last couple weeks of lacerations, including a couple by birds requiring stitches at the local hospitals in San Clemente and San Juan Capistrano.

There was also the incident of the old woman found in a ditch in San Juan Capistrano, and though the report didn't list the cause of death, it was thought to be natural causes. Even though the body was severely decomposed and found several days after the estimated time of death.

He then looked at the high school report. It was sketchy at best. Not much more to it than several phone calls received that students were attacked by a variety of birds and when the deputies arrived on the scene, a few students had some lacerations, but no birds were around except a few dead ones that had flown into the buildings.

He then picked up Chris' report about Rachel Tillinghast of Santa Ana being attacked by gulls and receiving several cuts. Chris also mentioned in the report Tory McKnight who was a student studying bird migration and nesting as assisting.

Finally, someone who witnessed an attack, and better yet, he had one authority on birds listed as well. Lt. Ferguson picked up the phone and called the Lifeguard Station and found out when Chris was on duty. They told Lt. Ferguson, Chris was there today and tomorrow from 9 until 4, then off for a day.

CHAPTER 7 – DAY 11

The evening before Tory told Chris about Dr. Bill Forrester coming. Chris had mixed emotions, though he tried not to show it. He and Tory had gotten much closer after the last couple days, and in spite of the bird business getting in the way of everything, he thought about asking her to stay with him for the night.

They had done some fairly serious and passionate kissing. But once Tory told Chris about her professor coming up, he figured the timing might not be proper. Especially as it had been Forrester's department that arranged for her to stay with the family in San Clemente in the first place.

Tory got the call from Dr. Forrester around 10:30 that morning, and they gathered at the pier in San Clemente. She saw him walking up from the base of the dock and went to greet him. After a slightly awkward handshake, she thanked him again for coming.

When he got Tory's phone call, part of the allure was to be on the beach again. He had been to San Clemente a few times and had always loved standing on the pier and looking out over the waves at the endless line of surfers floating on their boards. Forrester loved the sea and had told his family on several occasions that if he hadn't become a professor, he probably would be on a ship somewhere in the world. He was married to a psychologist, who was also a professor on campus. She always told him that the sea enamored most men.

It was why he took the chair at UCSD. San Diego was close to the ocean. So for the first fifteen minutes, they chatted about the area, his love of the sea and about how she was doing working with the zoological society, and other casual topics.

Tory had decided not to relay the conversation she had with Prof. Revere, as she didn't want him to know that she called her first. They finally turned to the purpose of his trip, and she explained as carefully she could, not wanting to put too much emotion into her report.

Dr. Forrester listened and nodded his head at specific points. When she explained how she questioned the events herself; he mostly stayed silent. At the end of her report, he said, "That is quite a story, not that I don't believe every word you say, but that is amazing that birds would approach without defending a nest or young, and in so many numbers."

She reiterated that she had looked around for any plausible explanation and found none. Dr. Forrester asked if he could meet the lifeguard who witnessed the girl's attack. He also would like to meet the homeless man who claimed to be assailed by a vulture.

"I know you can meet the lifeguard as I know exactly where to find him," and she pointed to Chris on his stand about two hundred yards from where they were standing. "I better come clean with something before you do, though."

Dr. Forrester looked at her, and she bit her lip as was her habit thinking how best to put things. "We are forming a relationship and are getting involved, so to speak."

Dr. Forrester laughed and said, she need not be so embarrassed about it, as he was not her father, and that he would probably approve in any event. Saving lives was always a noble profession in any form, and now he was even more anxious to meet whomever caught his best student's eye.

Tory blushed at the compliment and said, "Well then let's go see him." She walked toward the shore and explained how she got stonewalled at the high school. Dr. Forrester said a couple of well-placed calls might loosen that juggernaut.

As they reached the guard station, Chris had left his stand. They hadn't realized he saw a swimmer in trouble and had taken off to assist the young girl who was caught in a riptide and couldn't break free.

As he reached her, she was entirely out of breath and was struggling mightily. Chris pleaded with her to calm down. When she finally began to relax, he started swimming parallel to the shore as his training dictated until he was free of the riptide. He then began to swim to the shore until he knew that they could stand up. He then half-carried her to the beach, until her friend ran out and took her other side.

He gave her a quick check over once on the sand, declared her safe and sound and started back to the stand. When he saw Tory, he couldn't help but break

into a smile. Dr. Forrester walked up and shook Chris'
hand and said, "Nicely done," then to Tory said, "See?
How could anyone not like a person who saves others?"

Chris, who had been complimented many times
before about his duties took the comment in stride and
just mumbled a quick thanks.

Chris liked Dr. Forrester almost instantly. While the
man carried a severe look and demeanor, he was kind
and a good listener who rarely interrupted Chris, except
for points of clarification.

Chris relayed the story about Andy and explained
that apparently, his roommate had to call an ambulance
as Andy was very sick and taken to the hospital. He did
not know Andy's current condition, but he planned to
check on him soon. He talked about the incident with
Rachel and what he knew about South Beach and the
high school, which wasn't all that much.

"Has this, or anything like this, ever happened
before?" asked Dr. Forrester.

"Aside from gulls snatching food on occasion, I have
never seen or heard anything like this," answered the
lifeguard.

Forrester looked out over the ocean and just stared.
He had studied birds all his life and had never heard of
such bizarre behavior, let alone what could be the root
of it.

"Dr. Forrester? Earth to Dr. Forrester? Dr.
Forrester?" said Tory almost yelling the last.

"Oh...sorry, I was trying to remember if I had ever
run across any writings, or a thesis that talked about

changing the natural behavior of birds," he finally answered, "I can't think of anything that would shed any light on this."

Chris was absently looking out at the swimmers and surfers paying attention for trouble. Without looking at either of them, he asked, "What about Bodega Bay?"

"I thought about that," answered Dr. Forrester, "But we know nothing about that incident either. No one ever documented anything about the potential cause of that. It has become more urban legend than fact by now."

"Well it might be something to look into, even if it is only an incomplete report at best," responded Tory, "It could give us a starting place."

As they were debating the pros and cons of researching the Bodega Bay incident, a tall, balding man walked up to them. He produced his badge and announced his name to Chris and Tory in a congenial manner. "I'd like to talk with both of you for a few moments about some of the goings on around here," said Lt. Ferguson.

Tory answered, "I think I can guess the topic. And if I am right, you will want to include this man as well, Dr. Bill Forrester, the ornithologist from UCSD."

Lt. Ferguson smiled, shook his hand, and then Tory and Chris'. "Yes, you are right," Lt. Ferguson said, "Any enlightenment on this subject would help."

Chris radioed to the station that he was leaving his post so the other guards could keep an eye on his area while he was away. He grabbed his gear and asked, "Where do you want to talk?"

Lt. Ferguson pointed to the first restaurant at the beginning of the pier and said, "There would be fine."

As they reached the restaurant, Lt. Ferguson flashed his badge and asked the hostess for privacy. They went to a closed off outside patio, that would later open for the dinner rush.

When they sat down, Lt. Ferguson began asking them about Rachel, then Andy. After Chris had relayed both stories, they asked him about what happened at the high school. He said that they knew about as much as he did. He had read the report and not gotten much more from it.

It was Dr. Forrester who finally asked, "Obviously there must be more, or you wouldn't be trying to piece these incidents together. What else has happened?"

Lt. Ferguson smiled at the professor and said, "You should be in law enforcement. Okay, we have had another incident similar to the young man found in South Beach."

"Another body?" Chris asked incredulously.

"Three, on a charter fishing boat," answered Lt. Ferguson.

"My God," said Tory breathlessly, "And you think birds are involved?"

"I am beginning to think they are more than just involved. We can't find any other sign of foul play, and there were tracks all over South Beach and the boat. The bodies were decimated pretty much beyond recognition, and not a great deal of time had elapsed in either case," said Lt. Ferguson, "And by the way, this is not for public discussion, you three are now criminal consultants on this case, which is sensitive. I already have people breathing down my neck on this."

"I don't doubt it," replied Dr. Forrester, "Yeah, we understand about the confidentiality."

"So that taken care of, can any of you tell me what the heck is going on around here with these birds?" asked the lieutenant.

"Listening to the three of you," began Dr. Forrester, "all I can surmise is that there is something, maybe some disease taking place, that is affecting their behavior. That's as far as I can come up with."

"Oh great," complained Lt. Ferguson, "So now we have diseased birds committing murder." He shook his head.

"Hang on," protested Dr. Forrester, "I said it was a possibility, and only because nothing else makes sense."

"Especially when you add in the number of species involved," added Tory, "From seagulls to crows to vultures, and more."

"According to the report, there was a dead owl at the high school," said Lt. Ferguson, "In the middle of the afternoon, what could have made an owl join up with the other birds?"

"Do you have any of the birds from these attacks on ice anywhere?" asked Dr. Forrester hopefully, "We could run an autopsy on them."

"No such luck," said Lt. Ferguson, "They were swept up and disposed of at the high school, and no remains of birds at the other sights were found to pick up.

Makes me want to go on a little hunting spree though."

"No good," said Dr. Forrester, "Won't help unless you get lucky enough to bag the right bird to find the problem. It would be like shooting into a crowd hoping to hit a criminal."

"Yeah, but Andy was sure ready to try that tactic after his little incident," said Chris.

"Tell me what you know about that?" asked an interested Lt. Ferguson.

Chris retold the story and said that was the first of the attacks he had heard about or seen.

Lt. Ferguson said, "Perhaps I'll have to go to the hospital and talk with this guy Andy. He might be able to shed some light on this thing since he was an early report." And he made a note in his notebook.

Dr. Forrester said, "If it started with a turkey vulture, then that may be the carrier we would be looking for, first. Not that this makes things any easier. They are a rather shy bird and not the easiest to capture. Plus there are dozens around this area."

"Closer to a hundred I'd say," said Chris, "I have one tower alone with over thirty vultures on it by my house every day."

"Yes, that's right," said Tory excitedly, "Chris has the pictures, and besides the vultures, there were hundreds of other birds in a variety of species gathered around near them."

"I still have them on my phone," said Chris and he pulled the phone from his trunks and began flipping through the screen. "Yeah, here they are."

He showed the pictures to Forrester first who then passed them on to Ferguson. Forrester said, "This is very interesting and unusual."

Lt. Ferguson asked Chris, "Where did you say you lived?"

After Chris told him the lieutenant said, "That's interesting, we have another body from that town so badly decomposed that we thought she had been dead several days. She was from that same neighborhood."

"When I came out after sending the pictures to Tory, I pulled out to go to work, and they were all gone. I even went looking for them," said Chris. "Perhaps they went after her?"

"Well I believe we have someplace to start our search in any event," said Dr. Forrester, "If it is a pandemic, it had to start somewhere."

"But what about the high school and here at the beach?" questioned Tory, "Those birds couldn't have come from San Juan and attacked here? It's too far."

"Well if this is a disease and it is spreading rapidly, then we better act immediately. Before the whole area becomes affected," urged Dr. Forrester.

"Yeah, or infected," said Chris.

They agreed to meet early the next morning at Chris' house and see if they could determine anything from the roosting vultures.

Christy McNeil woke up for the second day in a row

with a sore throat. And this morning she had a terrible headache to go with it. I can't believe I am coming down with some stupid freaking bug, she said to herself.

She did not feel like getting out of bed, but she had a test today and couldn't miss it. She had to keep her grades high to remain a cheerleader, and she wanted to get into a decent college after SCHS.

She forced herself up and pulled on some clothes. As she pulled her shirt over her head, she brushed against one of the gashes she got from the birds at the high school the other day.

"Owww!" she said aloud.

"You okay sweetheart?" her mom called up the steps.

"Not really," complained Christy, "That stinking bird injury still hurts, and I don't feel well."

"Well come down here and let me take a look," her mother replied.

When Christy made it downstairs, her mother carefully looked at the top of her head where she had three cuts from the birds. Each one seemed bright red and slightly swollen.

"You DO know you are hurting me, right?" said Christy through clenched teeth.

"Oh, I am sorry dear, I barely touched them," her mom said, "But yes, they look inflamed, and I will make an appointment with the doctor this afternoon."

"Don't bother," snapped Christy, "It'll go away on its own."

"But they might be infected," said her mother with concern.

"Leave it be!" yelled Christy.

"Okay, fine," replied Helen McNeil. She had not known her daughter ever to be as cranky as she was this morning. "Now what would you like for breakfast? And do you want juice or milk?"

"Nothing!" Christy yelled again, "I don't feel good, and I can't swallow, so quit trying to force something on me."

"What's the matter, baby? What are your symptoms?" asked a now worried Helen.

"I just told you! I HAVE A FUCKING SORE THROAT AND A HEADACHE TO MATCH..."

"CHRISTY!" her mother yelled back, "Don't you ever swear at me and use that tone, I don't care how sick you are!"

Christy got up and stormed out the house without a word and headed for school. As she walked to the end of the second block, she got disoriented and confused. She rested for a moment against the traffic light, not sure where she was going or how to get there. She was still disoriented but eventually got her bearings and stepped off the curb against the light, right in the path of an oncoming car.

When Lt. Ferguson, Dr. Forrester, and Tory met at Chris' house, he was pointing to an empty tower. "I don't get it," Chris said with frustration, "They are always lined up there at this hour. On a day like this, they would already have their wings fanned out absorbing the sun and heat like a solar panel. Today, there isn't one."

"Is it possible, they took advantage of the thermals early?" asked Lt. Ferguson.

"The thermals aren't strong enough yet," answered Tory, "The heat hasn't built up enough. Plus they like to warm their wings and body first."

"She's right," said Dr. Forrester puzzled, "And we were all here early enough that they should have been communal roosting."

"Maybe they are out hunting?" said Chris.

"It is possible if they are flying low to the ground to pick up the scent of mercaptan, a gas produced by the beginnings of decay of dead animals, we might not see them," said Dr. Forrester. "But even so, they will wait until it is warmer, and the smells are stronger."

"You mean those things can smell?" asked Lt. Ferguson.

Tory answered before Dr. Forrester, "Most definitely. The part of its brain responsible for processing smells is particularly large, compared to other birds. Their heightened ability to detect odors allows them to find dead animals under a forest canopy or in thick brush."

"Well whatever they're doing, they are not doing it here," said Lt. Ferguson, "We might as well head out. Perhaps they found a new place to roost?"

Chris said, "May I suggest when you go, that you cruise by the greenbelt, just in case?"

"Fine idea," said Dr. Forrester. He looked at Tory

and said, "I'll go with Lt. Ferguson. Why don't you stay here with Chris in case they return, or if you see them, then you can call me." He winked at Chris.

"I have an hour before I have to get ready for work," Chris said, "I can make you some coffee."

Tory smiled at both men and said, "Well I guess I could stay for a cup."

As soon as Lt. Ferguson and Dr. Forrester left, Chris grabbed Tory and kissed her passionately. When they finally broke apart, Chris said, "I have been waiting to do that forever it seems."

"I know," said Tory apologetically, "I have been distracted since Dr. Forrester got here. The timing for all this sucks."

"No complaints." Chris laughed, "After all if all this wasn't going on, you and I might not get to spend nearly as much time together."

The birds they were looking for had in fact picked another place to roost that morning.

In Southern California, besides the buses in some communities, mass transportation took the form of a light rail train called Metrolink. The Orange County Line followed along the ocean from south of San Juan Capistrano all the way to Oceanside. Heading north, you could start the line in Oceanside and take it all the way to downtown Los Angeles. From there one could switch tracks and go most directions throughout

Southern California.

The San Juan Capistrano train station was very close to the Mission famous for the return of the swallows every March 19. It was a big deal when they returned it attracted a great many tourists to the area to watch the spectacle. Anyone watching the birds was fascinated how fast they could maneuver, change direction and sweep past them in their daring and continual rapid flight.

This particular morning there were a great many more birds in addition to the swallows. Surrounding buildings had dozens of birds on every roof. Every branch also had birds lined throughout the trees. And the species were as varied as the old adobe facades of each structure. One old restaurant shaped like boxcars had numerous vultures crowded along the apex of the roof-line. These birds were able to watch the comings and goings of the commuters in the parking lot but lost them as they got closer to the structure.

As was a regular weekday occurrence, people were awaiting the arrival of the train that had originated in Oceanside and was heading to Los Angeles. It would make almost a dozen stops after leaving the station weaving its way through Orange County.

Looking southward down the track, one could begin to see the train's headlights in the distance. As the crowd grew at the station, another large group was forming above them. Before too long the sky was filled with swallows darting through the air in an aerobatic display. In some places, the number of birds was so thick it was almost impossible to see through them. As the swarm got larger, it began to attract the attention of the ordinarily focused travelers.

A few people unsuccessfully tried to get pictures on their phones of the aerial circus above them, but the birds were both too small and too fast to get a clear shot.

Then it began.

The swallows began banking lower and lower until they were sweeping in and among the crowd. Several people struck by the birds and received scratches and cuts that soon started bleeding. The other birds took wing from their perches and joined in the melee with the swallows. These included the vultures along with mockingbirds, robins, pigeons, crows and more. All of them caught up in the cloud of birds circling in and through the crowd.

There were more strikes and soon people were running around frantically seeking protection from the attacks. It was too early for the shops to be open, so there was limited shelter from the onset of birds. By now, several people had gashes on their heads, arms, and legs. One man was using a briefcase to smack the birds as they flew toward him. He had successfully fended off several birds, but still was bleeding from the crown of his head.

About the time the swallows seemed to be lessening their persistent charges, a shadow fell over the station. People were horrified to look up and see numerous gulls and hawks circling tightly over the crowd.

Suddenly bells from the train crossing began to sound and the crossing gates lowered. People in the station thought this might be their opportunity to escape. As the train pulled into the station, it struck several birds, and the flock began to disband, with the birds flying higher to avoid the buildings and the train.

Once the train came to a full stop, the doors slid open, and people dashed into the cars for safety. This included several people who had not intended to board but sought the immediate shelter nonetheless. As they ran into the cars, the assault began again.

The birds sensing that they were about to lose their meal doubled their efforts under a single thought, Got to eat. Got to eat. GOTTA EAT! They flew into the train following the passengers and grabbed onto anyone they could find. The gulls were particularly vicious, as were the four hawks that joined them. They caused serious injury to two ladies who had run into the train ahead of them.

The doors began to slide closed, trapping people and birds together in the cars with no escape. The birds seemed not to care that they were also trapped and just continued with their assault on the passengers. Gotta Eat!

One of the ladies collapsed to the floor and was flailing with less energy than before. The lady, covered by numerous gulls, a Cooper's hawk, a mockingbird and even a dark-eyed junco that was pecking at her hand. Her hair was all over her face, which might have helped protect her face from worse damage. She screamed the whole while as she tried to fend off the attackers.

One of the two conductors ran into the car with a miniature California Angels bat. He struck as many birds as he could reach. He was doing a good job at slowing or stopping the onslaught, and after a while he had most of the birds removed from the passengers, including the woman. The conductor could still hear the screams and yells from the other cars and was trying to hurry to their aid. As the last of the birds were limping around the cabin, he said he had to help the other passengers and would return to check and administer to their wounds with a first aid kit very soon.

Some of the other passengers including those who had boarded in San Clemente and Oceanside were now gaining the upper hand, stomping or kicking any birds still moving around. One unusually large vulture had spread its wings as a threat, and the man with the briefcase took a long swing and knocked the bird over two rows of seats where it landed in a crumpled pile of feathers.

The passengers began helping each other to seats and dabbing the rivulets of blood from one another until more immediate help could arrive. The engineer had already called ahead to Irvine requesting medical assistance for the passengers. He also signaled the L.A. station master and advised her that the train would be delayed and why.

As Lt. Ferguson and Dr. Forrester were heading back to the station in San Clemente, Lt. Ferguson got a call on his cell phone. He listened to the report and asked a couple of questions including, "Where are they now?" and "How long can you hold them there?" After he hung up, he said to Dr. Forrester, "Well we found our birds. They just attacked a train and its passengers."

He called Chris and told him to hightail it to the Irvine Train Station so Tory could talk with the witnesses. Chris said he and Tory were already on their way. Lt. Ferguson put his car's emergency lights on and headed to the freeway.

Heather Mandeville had just gotten the fifteenth phone call that morning from parents reporting their children would be absent due to flu symptoms to San Clemente High School.

She called the vice principal's office and talked to his secretary about the reports. She was alarmed by the number of calls and thought perhaps it was time to advise the Center for Disease Control.

"How many from any one class?" asked Brooke Seymour, the vice principal's administrator.

"Not really that many from any one class, they seem to be all different classes, freshmen to seniors, and not from any particular classroom," replied Heather.

"Well you know the rules, only if there is ten percent of the entire school or 20 percent of a particular class do we report it to the CDC. Until we get to that level, we will treat it as normal absenteeism," said Brooke, "We have a lot farther to go to that ten or twenty percent."

"Yes, Ma'am," responded Heather. She had already regretted calling her for such a trifle as this.

Heather Mandeville later received a call about the death of one of the cheerleaders from the junior class who got struck by an automobile. She did pass that information onto Seymour, as well.

Meanwhile, doctors phones began ringing as adults set up appointments all over South Orange County requesting treatment for themselves, or their children, with everything from migraine headaches to fevers to sore throats and difficulty swallowing. Most convinced these were some form of the flu virus.

That same morning Rachel Tillinghast passed away. The reason given was respiratory failure due to head trauma and complications from influenza.

It was turning into a beautiful Friday in San Clemente. There wasn't a cloud in the sky, and it had already warmed to the low 70s with a mild breeze coming off the ocean. It would be a perfect day for walking around the town. The slope, already filled with shoppers and tourists heading toward the beach, was getting crowded.

It was the kind of weekend that many shop owners prayed for in San Clemente. And it was going to continue all the way through the festival next weekend. The weathermen were already calling for several days of sunshine and mild temperatures, even warmer than it had been this week so far. And although a week away, many thought the weather would happen as predicted.

Angie Johnson had been at her office arranging any advertising she possibly could and calling in as many favors as she had, along with promising more besides. She had to make next weekend's festival the best it had ever been. Angie loved doing events in San Clemente, and more often than not, they always had good weather. But she was hoping for what they called "Chamber of Commerce Weather" because it brought out the maximum number of tourists to the town.

Today, however, she had less joy for doing this than she usually did. She was threatened with losing her job as executive director for the Chamber of Commerce. If this event didn't come out as she projected, she would find herself unemployed in her beloved town.

That old bitch, thought Angie, *She has long outlived her welcome in the mayor's chair. They used to have the mayor's seat rotate among the city council each year. And the City Council itself was always voted into office. Somehow that had all changed. The Council seemed to vote themselves out of a job and in its place they voted for a mayor with a four-year term and no limits.*

She knew how it happened. It was David Irvin who spread his money to the right people and got the whole of the city charter changed at his command. Once done, he just let greed and power take its course, with his help, naturally. And now what remained of a once charming town with a fair government, was turned it into his own little corrupt country with his wicked witch of a daughter in charge.

She hoped that someday soon the citizens of San Clemente would come back to their lost senses and return to their former government before it was too late. But today, she was praying her position would remain intact and that the festival that lay before her would be as successful as she thought it could be.

It was something the local restaurateurs had come up with several years back. The city invited micro-brewers throughout the state to participate, and the festival had good results. Last year both sides of the pier were lined with portable tent canopies. People were rolling kegs and barrels up and down the pier, along with a bevy of sampling cups and assorted snacks to keep the thirst at a healthy level. The weather was nearly perfect all weekend long.

And even with the crowd that came and everything that went right, the Chamber missed their ticket sales projection by 15 percent or about 750 people. To hear the way their so-called mayor put it, one would think no one had shown up at all instead of having over 4.000 visitors.

This year's scheduled vendor turn out was already the best they had in the last few years, and Angie hoped the visitors would follow suit. According to the weather forecasters, they indeed wouldn't be able to blame the weather. She couldn't foresee anything going wrong with this festival if they could get a little extra push with the advertising.

She had already tapped the restauranteurs around town for little extra help, and she had pushed the local shopkeepers as hard as she dared. There were posters in every window. It was time to move on to other towns in the area to see if she couldn't persuade them in getting the word out. This tactic was always tricky as every borough had their own events and were trying to dissuade visitors away from one town to come to their own. After all, they had shops and restaurants, too.

As Angie called her counterpart in San Juan Capistrano, she heard the most shocking news. There was an attack on one of the trains by a massive flock of crazed birds Angie learned that many people were injured and they had to hold passengers because of the investigation and to tend to the wounded.

Apparently, the news corps was already out at Irvine interviewing and investigating the cause of the attack on the passengers. *Another bird incident*, thought Angie, and for once she agreed with her mayor. This type of press was the last thing they needed on the news for this week or next. And this time the national news had the story, not their local community. This attack could be just the type of thing that could sabotage the event and her plans. She hung up from her counterpart and turned on the first news station she came across.

There it was, a popular reporter talking to one of the train commuters. The person interviewed had several cuts across her face, and it looked like her scalp was cut and matted with blood also. She was talking about the crazed birds that flew right into the train cars and

continued the onslaught even after the train left the
station.

Then the camera panned to a scene of dead birds all
around the train car floor. They were praising a couple
of people for taking action fighting off birds in the car
and thwarting the attack.

Angie looked at the screen before her, "Where are
they all coming from, for Pete's sake? Look at how
many kinds of birds there are. What the heck is going
on around here? And why now?"

She watched in fascination as they went from one
person to the next to get their story. Nobody knew what
caused the birds go berserk, but all agreed that they
descended with a vengeance not seen in normal bird
behavior.

And of course, as there always was one in every
crowd, one crazy woman declared it was the end of the
world and the God had provoked the assault to warn
everyone to prepare.

ᖨ ᖨᐪᖨ ᖨ ᖨᐪᖨ ᖨᖨᐪᖨ ᖨᐪ ᖨᖨᐪᖨ ᖨᖨᐪᖨ ᖨᖨᐪᖨ

By the time Lt. Ferguson and Dr. Forrester arrived at
the Irvine train station, many of the victims had been
cleaned up and tended to. The train was released and
had continued on its appointed route. Most of the
commuters were waiting for the next train to get to
their planned destinations. Metrolink had taken all their
names promising them a free monthly railway pass for
their inconvenience.

To the side of the platform was a pile of birds. Lt. Ferguson tapped Dr. Forrester on the shoulder and pointed to the remains. "There's your autopsy pile, just waiting for you to figure this all out."

Dr. Forrester walked over to the mound and began poking through the birds to see if anything immediately stood out. An overzealous Metrolink agent came over to the professor and yelled, "Hey, you can't be touching those. Leave them alone."

Lt. Ferguson stepped up to the agent and flashed his badge saying, "He is a consultant with the Orange County Sheriff's Office and has full authority to review, and take, any of the remaining birds for evidence or further investigation."

The agent shrank under the forceful voice and size of Lieutenant Ferguson. The agent beat a hasty retreat back to his post. Dr. Forrester chuckled and said, "Well I hope you never have to use that tone on me!"

Lt. Ferguson smiled at him and said he had evidence gloves in his car and recommended that Dr. Forrester put some on before examining the bird's remains. After he retrieved some, he handed Dr. Forrester a pair of gloves and just said, "Good luck," and let Dr. Forrester continue his preliminary study of the birds.

A few moments later, Chris and Tory pulled up. They found Dr. Forrester still sifting through the remains and Lt. Ferguson talking with a few of the victims. Tory moved over to Dr. Forrester while Chris went to hear what the lieutenant was learning about the attack.

Tory asked Dr. Forrester if the professor noticed

anything unusual.

"Not a damn thing," said Dr. Forrester disgustedly, "Other than they seem particularly well fed, no marks, or discharge, no scratches or cuts, except blunt trauma from hitting them like a baseball. Numerous broken necks, etc., but nothing to indicate what changed their behavior."

"Look at all the different species," said Tory in amazement, "Swallows, juncos. sparrows, vultures, doves. My God, there is even a killdeer over there. How can they all be infected?"

"No idea," said Dr. Forrester shaking his head, "I have never known or heard of any disease, or behavior, crossing so many lines."

"So what now?" asked Tory.

"I am going to take at least one of each species down to UCSD for an autopsy and to run tests," he answered, "Care to help me load up? But get some gloves from the lieutenant before you touch them."

"If it is all right with you, I would also like to send off a few of these specimens to Cornell, just for a second opinion?" asked Tory.

"Ellen Revere?" questioned Forrester.

Tory nodded nervously. "I told her I would keep her in the loop," she said apologetically.

"No harm there. Prof. Revere is a great lady, and her help might be invaluable," said Dr. Forrester, "Besides, Cornell has more toys than we do, and may get answers quicker. Good thinking, Tory. There is also someone at the SD Zoological Society I may send a couple of these to as well."

"If time is of the essence, any help could be invaluable," agreed Tory, "But thanks for your encouragement."

Lt. Ferguson and Chris were not getting very far with the witnesses to the situation. They heard over and over again that the birds just began swarming like a cloud of insects, and then advanced without provocation. It didn't seem to matter what kind of bird it was, they all acted like they were starving and wanted to peck the skin right off their bones.

One lady who was still extremely distraught was saying how they kept trying to aim for her eyes. "It's like it was the only thing they wanted to do was poke my eyes out," she said and then began crying again. Luckily, she only had a couple of scratches on her face and no damage to her eyes themselves.

"If it hadn't been for the conductor and that guy with the briefcase, I don't know that I could have gotten them all off me," one man said, "They just kept coming at me from all directions. I have scratches all over me, and they are itching and burning like crazy. The medics put some medicine all over me, but it hasn't helped, yet. It's about to drive me nuts."

Chris told him that he felt bad for him, but was sure that the itching would eventually subside.

Lt. Ferguson caught up with the man with the briefcase who now had his arm in a sling. The lieutenant asked about his injury, and the man laughed saying he got a little over ambitious with a vulture and apparently pulled a tendon in his shoulder from hitting the damn thing so hard. The medics had wanted to take him to the hospital, but he refused further treatment.

"I got to tell you, deputy, I have never seen such bizarre behavior before, and I see a lot of weird shit on the internet," he was saying to Lt. Ferguson, "These birds were on a mission, though I am not sure what the mission was. At first I thought they were just panicking being trapped inside the train, but these birds were on a mission. They were out to do as much damage as they could. I just don't get it."

"Well thank you for helping your fellow passengers out," Lt. Ferguson said.

"The truth is, I think I just became obsessed with taking as many of those damn things out before they could get to me," he said with a smirk.

"Whatever the reason, you helped a good many people from becoming more seriously injured," smiled Lt. Ferguson, "Although I appreciate your candor."

Lt. Ferguson got several more pair of examination gloves from his cruiser, and they loaded about twenty birds into a vinyl bag in Lt. Ferguson's trunk. Then the four of them left the scene and headed back. Chris was already late for work, though he called ahead and said he might not make it in until this afternoon.

When they returned to Chris' home, Dr. Forrester asked Tory if she wanted to return to the campus with him. She thought about it and said, "I think it best if I stay up here so I can monitor the situation. Also, we need to find the carrier of whatever it is you find in these birds, and I agree to look for a vulture."

"It might be in the trunk now. I am hoping so, but you are probably right. These attacks are far from over, I fear there are going to be more," Dr. Forrester said resignedly, "I'll keep you up to speed with whatever we find, and I'll get those specimens off to Cornell for you and the SD Zoo. You call Prof. Revere and let her know they are coming. Give her my regards when you do."

"Will do, and thanks," said Tory, "And not just for this, but for believing me. It means a great deal."

Dr. Forrester smiled at his student and said, "Keep up the good work, but you guys be careful. We are still no closer to knowing what is causing this or how many birds could be affected. And if you go looking too hard for trouble, it may find you."

After putting the birds in the trunk, he got into his car and pulled out his phone. He set up a lab schedule with a couple of students before pulling away.

Lt. Ferguson also said goodbye and promised to let them know about his visit with Andy, and if anything else came up. "Let's hope they got their fill of attacking folks for a while," he said, although he suspected down deep that wasn't true.

By that afternoon, because there was no loss of life or severe physical damage, the news story about the bird altercation was relegated to a bizarre human interest story. Little would be remembered in a day or two about the "crazed San Juan birds" as they were called.

It was even difficult to find much about it on the

internet.

K ← ← K ← ← K ← ← K ← K ← ← K ← ← K ← ←

"This is very odd," said Jackie Larger, the nurse practitioner at the San Clemente Urgent Care Center, "We haven't seen hardly any cases of flu or strep this year. And it is kind of late to begin cropping up. Let's take a closer look."

Nurse Larger asked Larry Hassle to open his mouth wide and looked down his throat. While it looked inflamed, she could not see any infection or signs of strep or tonsillitis.

After she finished her examination, Larry said, "And this headache is enough to make me crazy. I feel angry all the time since I began getting this. But I can't even take a drink to calm down because my throat hurts and I choke when I try."

Nurse Larger checked his pulse, heart, and lungs. His blood pressure was a little high, but he had shown that in previous visits, so she wasn't too concerned about it. Everything else seemed mostly normal.

"I don't know Mr. Hassle, I can prescribe some antibiotics to see if that can help, but unless more symptoms show up, the only thing I can see is that you have an elevated temperature and some inflammation in your throat, but I do not see anything else. Were you bitten by an insect or animal lately? Or have you eaten anything you could be allergic to?"

"No, well, I got pecked by a bird almost a week ago,

left a nasty cut on my arm," and he rolled up his sleeve to show her the remnants of a small cut as he finished saying this.

"Well it looks a little red, and I'll have them put an analgesic on it, but that's nothing that would have anything to do with your other symptoms, especially if it's from a bird," Nurse Larger said.

This scene was being played out at multiple doctors offices around the area. The ailments were similar. Some patients had higher temperatures and worsening symptoms. Other patient's reactions were frustration and pain. In several instances, it got the better of their senses, and they lashed out verbally, and a couple even physically, after the vague prognosis.

ᴋ ᴋᵗᴋ ᴋ ᴋᵗᴋ ᴋ ᴋᵗᴋ ᴋ ᴋᵗ ᴋ ᴋᵗᴋ ᴋ ᴋᵗᴋ ᴋ ᴋᵗᴋ

Dr. Bennett was summoned back to the morgue to be the Medical Examiner for a tragic accident involving a high school student and a speeding car.

He stood over Christy McNeil and began his inspection. He already knew the cause of death was blunt trauma to the head and he thought the mortuary was going to have a tough time making her bashed face look normal again.

He began the process of cutting open her skull to see how much damage resulted from the moment the car struck her. As he peered into the cranium, he looked at Christy's brain and saw something quite odd. The doctor looked again and saw increased intracranial pressure due to a rise in the cerebrospinal fluid.

This is the fluid that surrounds the brain and spinal cord. This was very rare for someone of Christy's age. He thought to himself, *It looks like a case of encephalitis. But that virus frequently attacked only the very young or very old. Rarely was it seen in a usually healthy adult or teen?*

Dr. Bennett began looking for bite marks or signs of a particularly nasty mosquito bite or tick. He saw some small cuts on her scalp which he first thought might be due to the car accident. He looked at them again and realized they had occurred earlier. Well before the crash, but probably within the last several days to a week.

The cuts seemed inflamed and possibly infected, but this was not the wound he was seeking. He could tell what caused them from their appearance. He had seen his share of bird beak cuts this past week, and he correctly assumed this must have been one of the high school kids attacked by the birds Lt. Ferguson told him about earlier.

He saw nothing like a bite mark on her anywhere. He began thinking what else might cause encephalitis and ran through the checklist in his mind crossing off each possibility as soon as he thought of them, *Measles? No. Mumps? No. Rubella? No. Rabies? Apparently not. Eastern Equine Encephalitis Virus? Highly doubtful. West Nile? Hmm, possibly, but there haven't been any reported cases this year. And that would occur more in summer and early fall, when mosquitoes are active, although it could have incubated over the last several months.*

As Dr. James Bennett continued to debate with himself over the cause of the brain swelling, he examined her brain and spinal cord more closely. He needed to see how far the virus might have progressed, as symptoms of encephalitis could contribute to her death.

His first job was to determine a cause of death, which he already knew. Figuring out how she got that way could take much longer to establish.

He would have to talk with the girl's mother to check out any other possible symptoms. This conversation was not one he was looking forward to, but it might be the only way to determine what might have happened to the girl.

CHAPTER 8 – DAY 12

The next day the floodgates opened. Patients showed up at every hospital and urgent care facility all over Orange County, mainly as most doctor's offices were closed for the weekend. Disorientation, confusion, low- and mid-grade fevers, muscle weakness, speech problems, choking from eating or drinking anything, was just the start of the list of ailments. A few were exhibiting an unnatural fear of water or fluids, while at the same time complaining of voracious appetites. The ambulances began also arriving, bringing people who had fallen unconscious or were having convulsions.

The Orange County medical community had never seen anything like this before. The same questions kept being asked in every medical facility and almost always with the same negative result:

Did the patient fall or hit their head on something?

Any animal or insect bites occur lately?

Had they ingested something not generally in their diet?

Has the person had any recent injuries from an accident?

A couple of people had mentioned the cuts from being attacked by a bird, but these were immediately dismissed or only given a cursory glance.

Some complained about a sore stomach along with

their constant hunger, but those went down a completely different path from anything relating to their other symptoms.

Most of the patients were prescribed antibiotics and told to go home, that there was little they could do for them unless their symptoms worsened. There were some blood or urine tests, but these were always negative and ineffective against neural diseases, so they showed no problems.

Only one doctor in all of Orange County had seen this type of problem first-hand before. He had practiced in Africa under the Doctors Without Borders for three years. He set up an office in Dana Point after his tour with them. He helped out at an urgent care center one Saturday a month.

Doctor Terry Dorsey had seen this with the villagers in Nigeria. Cathy Blanchard didn't have any noticeable insect or animal bites but claimed all the symptoms of having an advanced case of rabies. This prognosis made no sense to Dr. Dorsey. There was no cause that he could understand for her ailments.

The first symptoms of rabies are very similar to those of the flu, including general weakness or discomfort, fever, and headache, which she listed. These symptoms typically last for days, but in Cathy's case she said they only began the day before yesterday, starting with a sore throat and difficulty swallowing, but she also complained of unending hunger.

The last was the only symptom that didn't fit the standard profile. Dr. Dorsey felt that ailment was because Cathy was complaining about choking when trying to drink and hadn't eaten properly due to it.

There were prickling and itching sensations at the site of a cut on her scalp that she received from a seagull that pecked at her while at the beach in San Clemente. That was the only outwardly sign of any external damage. Through their discussion, Dorsey surmised that she also seemed to be progressing rapidly into symptoms of cerebral dysfunction, anxiety, confusion, and agitation.

Dorsey guessed that these might soon develop into delirium, abnormal behavior, hallucinations, and insomnia. That is if the patient lasted that long, which wasn't a sure bet if he was right.

He knew that the acute period of the disease typically ended after 2 to 10 days. He also knew that once the clinical signs of rabies appear, the disease was nearly always fatal, and any treatment was typically supportive at best. Once a person began to exhibit symptoms of the disease, survival was all but impossible.

Disease prevention included administration of both passive antibody, through an injection of human immune globulin and a round of vaccinations with rabies vaccine. And that had to happen almost immediately after whatever caused the infliction.

Dr. Terry Dorsey thought about all this, including the several patients he watched die from the disease in Nigeria.

"Cathy, I know this may sound a bit strange, but you

seem to have all the symptoms of contracting the rabies virus, and I want to begin an immediate regiment of rabies vaccine," he said with great concern.

"I thought you could only get rabies from an animal bite?" she asked the doctor, "Nothing bit me!"

"Very rarely a case could be transferred through the air, but usually that requires an enclosed environment with infected animals, like in a cave or other tight space," the doctor said. While sure of his prognosis, he was grasping at straws to explain how she got it.

"I haven't been spelunking lately, doctor," she said sarcastically, "And I don't have any rabid animals cuddling up with me at night."

"Nonetheless, I want to start treatment immediately, this is very serious Cathy, and if I am right, you don't have any time to lose," Dr. Dorsey insisted.

"And if you are wrong?" Cathy asked.

"Well, rabies injections are anything but comfortable. However, they are not detrimental if I am wrong. But I saw this many times before, and everything you are complaining about leads me to be pretty certain you somehow contracted this virus, although I admit I am not sure how," he finished.

Cathy stared at the doctor, but finally caved in and said, "All right, but I would like more proof."

"And you will have it, I am going to run a couple of tests, and I am afraid those won't be pleasant either although necessary," the doctor said apologetically, as he ordered a nurse to prepare the first injection of the vaccine.

"What kind of tests?" asked Cathy suspiciously.

"A spinal tap first and foremost," answered Dr. Dorsey.

Cathy was scheduled for the tests on Monday. She would be one of the few patients seen that day that had so much as a fighting chance for survival.

Jean Turkovitch spent most of her day venting poison over her phone at the useless public servants of San Juan Capistrano for allowing this stupid bird story to go over the airwaves. She was at last beginning to breathe normally again.

The story had faded from the top and seemed to be falling lower with each hour and day that passed. *Thank God the newspeople realize what an insignificant deal this is,* she thought. It could have ruined all her plans for the festival.

As it was, she was pleased with the amount of attention the festival was getting, and she was scheduled to do two interviews next week with local TV stations. Convinced as she was the only one who was going to make this event a success.

I am not going to let anything stand in the way of this, she thought. *Especially not these fucking birds.*

Across town, Angie was trying to calm her counterpart down, and undo the damage their mayor did with her last phone call.

"Linda, you know Turkovitch, she is just that way.

She seems convinced that our whole town will slide into the ocean if she isn't here to keep it in place," pleaded Angie on the phone.

"She has no right to scream at me that way," Linda said, "She acted like I caused the stupid birds to go after those people. It's not the kind of publicity we look for either, but instead of having any sympathy, she just screamed at me and acted like it was my fault."

Angie knew from experience the best way to handle Linda Mayhew was to let her spout and get it out of her system. Although, Linda was more upset than Angie had ever seen her over this turn of events.

Angie, at last, realized that there was an undertone to Linda's speech. It was fear.

"Linda, do the authorities have any idea what caused this bird incident?" asked Angie.

"They haven't said anything to us if they do," said Linda and then after a pause, "Angie, this has been taking place all over town. Nothing as big as this was, but people are being dive-bombed by birds everywhere. There is hardly a street that is safe from these birds. And all kinds, too, just like this morning. We don't know what could be causing it, but our City Council is being called into a special session on Monday to try and figure out how best to handle this."

"I'm sure it is just a phase of the moon or something causing this," said Angie trying to calm Linda, "It always seems to be something to make our jobs more interesting."

Linda finally chuckled at the last comment and said,

"Yeah, just when you thought they threw everything at you to make your position impossible enough."

After saying goodbye to Linda, Angie thought about the stories she had heard around her town, too. It seemed that there was more every day and the attacks were getting worse and more frequent. Only HER city was squashing any discussions about it, rather than gathering any help to see how to stop it.

She also knew it was happening in other nearby towns like Dana Point and Capistrano Beach. She wondered what they might be doing about it and thought about calling her friends at Dana Point to ask.

She stood up and walked to the window. As she looked out over the street, a bird struck her window squarely and made Angie jump backward and nearly fall over a chair.

She came back to the window and saw a Mockingbird laying on the walkway. It appeared dead from the collision, with its head facing backward in an unnatural pose.

"What the hell is going on?" Angie asked herself out loud.

CHAPTER 9 – DAY 14

Jimmy Clowe was back at his doctor's office to receive his second injection of rabies vaccine from Boomer. As he was checked out by his doctor, she wasn't at all pleased with the results of the first shot. Jimmy shouldn't be showing any signs of advancement, and instead, he had a low-grade fever, and there were some irritation and prickling around the bite area. It was redder and more inflamed than it should have been. The doctor hoped for better results with the second injection.

ᛕᛕᛕᛕ ᛕᛕᛕᛕ ᛕᛕᛕᛕᛕ ᛕᛕᛕᛕ ᛕᛕᛕᛕ ᛕᛕᛕᛕ

Monday morning at the laboratory at UCSD, Bill Forrester was examining some of the birds that he brought back from Orange County. He had two grad students working with him, and Ashley Gallt was examining two of the swallows, while Dennis Tye was performing a pathology on the turkey vulture with Dr. Forrester.

Blood tests showed a virus, but nothing listed among the known viral maladies in birds. They specifically checked for Avian Influenza and some of the other known diseases, especially anything that would cross various species as this did.

The virus was lost on Dr. Forrester. Nothing was cataloging in the research he checked.

"There seems to be a great amount of food in the stomach and intestines of all these animals," commented Ashley, "Is it possible that they ingested some new germ that spread into their system?"

"We are finding different contents in different birds," said Dennis, "As expected, they have dissimilar diets."

"Except for the fact they were all eating a goodly amount of carnivorous matter," said Dr. Forrester, "Most of them have a good deal more than insects mixed in there. The question is why would they change their diet and eat things they are normally deathly afraid of?"

"Safety in numbers?" questioned Ashley, "No, that makes no sense, most of these birds would be fearful of the other bird species as well."

"What would cause them to flock and attack together?" asked Dr. Forrester rhetorically, "The answer has to be in this mysterious virus."

They had sent samples down to the Zoology Department at the university, along with specimens to the San Diego Zoological Veterinary Laboratory. Perhaps they might have an answer by now, and Dr. Forrester thought about calling them to compare notes.

He no more made that thought and the phone rang in his office. He answered it, "Bill Forrester" and then heard another colleague on the other line.

"Hello Ellen, did you get a chance to examine the samples I sent?" asked Dr. Forrester. After a long pause, he said, "How can that possibly be? That has only been done in a laboratory setting, and never seen in the field."

After a few minutes of discussion he finished the phone call with, "Okay, that would be great, thanks. If what you are saying is true, we have a bigger problem than we originally thought, and it was pretty huge already. I will see you later today." He hung up his office phone.

After a moment Dr. Forrester said, "Well, we now have a bigger problem than attacking birds. Dennis, call the zoology departments and have them check those blood samples for a similar strain against rabies."'

"Uh, Dr, Forrester, birds don't carry rabies," he cautiously replied.

"Wrong tense, Dennis. You mean they didn't carry rabies. Prof. Ellen Revere from Cornell seems to think they have developed a viral strain of their own. And she is so certain of this that she is flying out here today to compare notes."

"How would they contract it, they have no salivary glands? And if anything bit them they would die from the bite before the disease could infect them," argued Ashley.

"Apparently Prof. Revere is convinced this is an entirely new strain of the virus and may even be subject to airborne infection or shared meals, or both," finished Dr. Forrester.

Dennis was already on the phone and was getting some crude flack from the other department.

Dr. Forrester walked over and took the phone and spoke into the receiver, "This is Dr. Bill Forrester, head of the Ornithology Department, and it is me who has made this request. And yes I know, birds don't carry rabies, but I want you to compare this to all your known strains. It is likely to be slightly different, and we need to know what those differences are. Cornell has already identified this, and we are lagging behind them, so hop to it unless you want this new strain to carry Cornell's I.D. on it instead of ours." He then hung up the phone.

"That ought to get them moving, they hate losing to another college to be first in a discovery." He smiled as he said this knowing he felt the same.

ᐠ ᐠᐟ ᐠ ᐠᐟ ᐠᐟ ᐠ ᐠᐟ ᐠᐟ ᐠ ᐠᐟ ᐠᐟ ᐠ ᐠᐟᐟ ᐠ ᐠᐟᐟ ᐠ ᐠᐟ ᐠ ᐠᐟᐟ ᐠ ᐠᐟᐟ

That same morning, Dr. Jerry Dorsey was on the phone with the assistant deputy director of the Center for Disease Control or CDC as it is better known.

After identifying his fourth case of rabies at his office, he knew he had to raise the alarm. Something was going on, and it wasn't right.

He spoke to Dr. Anna Lanz, MD MPH and was trying to convince her that some rabid epidemic was taking place in his town even though he didn't know the cause.

"Perhaps it isn't zoonotic in nature, doctor," she tried to reason with Dr. Dorsey.

"Doctor Lanz, I spent three years over in Africa, and I am telling you. These patients have all the symptoms of rabies infections, even if they don't exhibit the visible result of an animal bite. It is there just the same," he pleaded to his skeptic.

"Have you checked any of them for signs of Encephalitis or given them a spinal?" asked Dr. Lanz.

"The first two are going in for both tests today," he acknowledged, "I couldn't get the other two in until tomorrow."

"Well after the test results are in, you can call me and let me know the findings, whether you are right or not. But I must say I suspect you will find another problem besides rabies," Dr. Lanz said, then dismissively, "Thank you for contacting the CDC," and was gone.

Great she thinks I'm looney tunes, thought Dr. Dorsey. *Of course, it's not that I haven't wondered about this myself. If I could only figure out what the legitimate cause was of this disease?*

$$\kappa \leftarrow^{\leftarrow} \kappa \leftarrow^{\leftarrow} \kappa \leftarrow^{\leftarrow} \kappa \leftarrow^{\leftarrow} \kappa \leftarrow^{\leftarrow} \kappa \leftarrow^{\leftarrow} \kappa \leftarrow^{\leftarrow}$$

Chris had learned about Andy from Lt. Ferguson Saturday afternoon. He was upset that he didn't take Andy's concerns more seriously. Though he knew he wasn't responsible for his death, he still felt guilty for not helping him seek medical attention earlier. It might have made a difference.

After being off Sunday, Chris came to his station that morning to a frightening sight. Washed up all over the beach were about two dozen dead seagulls. He didn't touch them as he was suspicious that they were probably diseased in some way. He also warned anyone on the beach of the same thing.

He called Tory, who in turn phoned Dr. Forrester. Dr. Forrester said he would send his two students to pick up the birds for examination. He also told Tory about his conversation with Prof. Revere.

"A new strain of rabies? How is it possible? Only mammals carry that disease," she said.

"They ran tests several years ago in a laboratory and successfully introduced the virus into birds, though it was through injection," answered Dr. Forrester, "Apparently this might be some new strain that is transferred through shared food, or possibly even airborne, if in close enough proximity. It is certain enough to get Ellen Revere on a plane heading for here, today."

"That would also explain why different species began congregating together. If they shared the same disease, they wouldn't be right in the head. Did one of the test birds escape? Do you believe there is a carrier causing this? How about the turkey vulture?" thought Tory out loud in rapid speech.

"I am at a loss about that. I know all the test birds were destroyed years ago, and no, I don't believe any escaped. It is possible that this is a migrating or transient bird passing through the area. It may be dead already, although carriers seldom exhibit, or succumb, to symptoms. This may be a bigger problem than we suspected," said Dr. Forrester, "Think of all the birds that not only could be infected but can and will infect others. Not to mention all the attacks that have taken place already."

"Do you think they might spread the virus to people, too?" asked a horrified Tory.

"I believe it is more than a fifty-fifty chance they already have," said Dr. Forrester, "We may want to contact the local hospitals and urgent care centers to see if they have any unusual cases they are working on, and what is the cause they attributed to them."

"Dr. Forrester, if this is all true, how can we contain this?" asked Tory.

"I am not sure. I am still trying to digest the horror of the possibility of having an entire new rabies strain spread through millions of birds in the U.S. And that doesn't even take in the idea of the species that migrate great distances each year, possibly spreading this disease to other continents."

"Talk about your nightmare pandemic scenario," Tory said breathlessly, "I will do a quick look-up on the virus and get to know the symptoms and signs, as this is a mammalian problem.. Then I will begin checking with the hospitals."

"Hopefully I am wrong about this," said Dr. Forrester, "Rabies is nearly always fatal if not treated in time. And if the medical profession doesn't understand what they are looking for, it may be too late for many of them."

"Oh my God, Andy!" yelled Tory.

"I'm sorry, what?" asked a stunned Dr. Forrester.

"Chris told me Andy died! They said it was due to

exposure and the flu, but I'll bet if they did an autopsy, they would find a different cause. He was one of the very first to be attacked by a vulture." said Tory.

"Get on this and convince them to check for encephalitis," said Dr. Forrester, "I'll bet that may have caused the respiratory problems. Prof. Revere and I will get up there as soon as we possibly can."

Dr. Forrester wished Tory luck and hung up.

Tory thought about what might happen if she called the hospitals. She remembered her reception at the high school, and how quickly they dismissed her. In her mind, she thought she had a better idea.

She punched up Lt. Ferguson's number.

"Hello Tory," he answered, "Have we any news on the birds we collected?"

"Boy do we," answered Tory, and went into the conversation she just had with Dr. Forrester. When she had brought Lt. Ferguson up to speed, she said, "I thought it might be easier to convince people and get answers if you would call the hospitals, instead of a grad student from UCSD."

"I might even be able to do that one better," said Lt. Ferguson, "Come on down to the station, and we will go see the medical examiner and have him do the legwork on this. He can talk medical jargon with these folks. They may listen to him more than they would either a grad student or a cop."

"I'll head right over," said Tory. As she headed for her Jeep, she called Chris and apprised him of the situation.

"We are going to have to call everyone attacked and

inform them to get checked out for rabies, like the passengers on the train," said Chris, "Plus we have to find a way to stop these things from attacking people."

"And just what bright idea do you have for that?" asked Tory,

"None at the moment," said Chris disheartened, "How soon will those classmates of yours get here to clean up this mess on my beach?"

"Hopefully not long, but make sure no one messes with those birds. We don't know how pathogenic that virus is, and we sure as hell don't want to compound the problem," said Tory.

"I hear that," answered Chris, "By the way, are we on for dinner tonight?"

"Let me find out what the plans are with Dr. Forrester and Prof. Revere before I answer that, but that sounds nice," said Tory.

She was now speeding her way to the San Clemente Police Station.

Dr. James Bennett was back in the morgue reexamining the young girl with new marching orders. He had noticed the swelling of the brain on Friday and saw that there might be problems with the spinal fluid. He was now going over the victim for distinguishing signs of rabies.

He had sent fluid from the brain and spine to pathology to check for viral infection. They had promised him results by 10:00 that morning, and it was only 9:15. Dr. Bennett was in a hurry, as he knew Lt. Ferguson would be bursting in any minute wanting answers.

He called the lab and asked for an update. They told him what he suspected, although they could not determine any actual signs of a cause. As he hung up the phone, Joe Ferguson and a pretty young lady walked through the double doors of the morgue.

Lt. Ferguson, barely remembering his manners, introduced Tory to Dr. Bennett and then said, "Well?"

Pointing at the corpse on the table, the doctor said, "If this young lady is any indication of what you told me, then your investigation is spot-on. She was struck and killed by a car, but she has, or I should say, had, encephalitis and a viral infection in her cerebrospinal fluid. I think that is why she stepped out in front of oncoming traffic. She was confused and disoriented and could not reason."

"So a rabies infection killed her?" asked Tory.

"Only circumstantially," explained Bennett, "Once a rabies virus begins to assert itself in the nervous system, it begins to cause swelling of the brain and spinal fluids."

"I understand about encephalitis, doctor," she interrupted, "What I meant was how it could develop so quickly? From what I read, rabies can take months or years to develop to such an advanced state. The high school event is just a few days old. Did you find any other wounds besides the one on her head?"

"No, and in speaking to the girl's mother, she couldn't remember any complaints from her daughter previously. She also said her daughter had acted extremely agitated, and swore at her, which she had never done before. She said an animal had never bitten her daughter in her life."

"Is there anything else that could cause these symptoms beyond rabies?" asked Lt. Ferguson.

"Many things, but they make even less sense than getting rabies from a bird," Dr. Bennett answered, "and I checked into all of them to make sure, and everything but a rabies virus falls apart. Plus, that is what shows up in the blood and fluids, although it is a mutated strain, according to the lab. And there's one more thing."

"What's that?" asked Lt. Ferguson.

"Let's not forget our other contestants around here. This could explain the attacks on them and how they managed to perform such acts of savagery in a short time," Dr. Bennett said.

"I already made that connection," said the lieutenant, "It's what to do about it that concerns me."

Tory and Lt. Ferguson spoke to the M.E. about relating his findings to local hospitals and urgent care centers and convincing them to watch for any possible symptoms of rabies that might come in.

"If this virus works anywhere this fast as it did on her, then I am sure they already have seen some patients," the doctor said, "Problem would be if they didn't know what to look for, they may have turned them away. But yeah, I'll begin making calls, and I'll include the CDC on that list. They have more resources than I do."

"Good idea," replied Lt. Ferguson, "We will be heading to the beach. Apparently, Tory's boyfriend has seen more than a dozen birds wash up on the shore this morning."

"Bag me one, if you can," said Dr. Bennett, "I'd like to do some tests on it here and get a closer look at this strange virus."

"Will do," said Ferguson. As they turned to go, the lieutenant stopped and asked the doctor, "Jim, do you think in any way this could be airborne?"

"Let's pray that it is not," Bennett answered, "If it is we have a helluva mess. I am holding onto the fact that the victim was attacked by a bird, even if no saliva transmission was involved. Although I would like to look closer at the virus before ruling it out."

Ferguson nodded and mumbled a quick thanks and left.

Upon arriving at the beach, they saw Chris running back and forth on the sand and flailing his red lifeguard warmups. They saw birds flying all around and realized as they got closer that other seagulls had moved into the area and were trying to take scraps from a pile of birds stacked close to Chris' station.

Tory immediately ran to the station and began yelling and waving her arms as well to chase the birds away.

Lt. Ferguson decided to let them handle the attackers

and readied his pistol should the need for stronger measures arise.

Chris yelled to Tory as she approached, "They started showing up shortly after I called you. They are eating the dead birds like they were served lunch."

Tory yelled back to him, "These dead birds probably have the rabies virus, and it may transmit the disease if they feed on them."

The gulls weren't going to give up easily. The sight of so much meat in simple grasp kept them determined. Many of them were already infected. All they could concentrate on was Gotta eat!

The others that weren't infected gave up and left the area for easier pickings.

As Lt. Ferguson approached Chris, he pointed his revolver to the aggressive birds and asked, "Should I increase your pile there?"

Tory yelled from the other side, "Wait, you don't know that they are infected! There is no reason to start killing birds that are just doing what they normally do."

"Care to tell that to that young girl's mom? How about Andy? Let's get him down here and ask him. Oh wait, we can't, can we?" growled Lt. Ferguson. "Meanwhile, what if they ARE infected? Is there some litmus test we can run to find out?"

"Easy, Lt. Ferguson," pleaded Chris, "Tory's right, we can't be blasting up the beach without knowing which birds are a problem and which aren't."

"I have a whole morgue full of people that are there because of these birds, and now we could be facing a far worse problem if they are infecting other people. I view this as public safety, pure and simple." Lt. Ferguson lined up one particular gull in his sights and felt his finger begin to pull back the trigger.

"Hang on, if you discharge your weapon on an open beach, there are going to be inquiries and possible actions against you," implored Chris, "And we need you too badly to be on administrative leave!"

Lt. Ferguson hesitated then released the trigger and holstered his gun. Instead, he brought out his taser and immediately shot a bird that was ripping intensely into one of the dead birds. He watched as the bird violently shook for a moment, then fell lifeless, itself.

"One down," he smirked and turned to Chris.

The electric shock and noise seemed to carry through to the other birds and caused several more gulls to fly off to safety.

Tory walked up to Lt. Ferguson and Chris and said, "Good thinking, and thanks. I wouldn't want to have anything happen to our one friend on the force in this whole mess."

Lt. Ferguson smiled at her and said, "I have a feeling you are going to have a lot of friends when word of this gets out. Speaking of which, I need to get back to the station and get the ball moving."

Tory turned to Chris and said, "I am sure you had no choice, but I assume you handled all these birds and stacked them here?"

"As you said, I had no choice as they were all over the beach and the other birds started to show up in mass. I couldn't possibly keep them all away with them spread out all over. I still had a pair of the evidence gloves Lt. Ferguson gave me, and I made sure I washed thoroughly afterward. I held my breath when I was near or holding them," he answered her.

"Well we need to bag a couple for our M.E.. He wants to run some tests of his own," said Lt. Ferguson, "I'll get some more gloves and bags." He headed back to his car parked in the emergency vehicle area.

"Do you think they all died from the rabies virus?" Chris was now asking Tory.

"I had looked up the Bodega Bay incident, and if this is in any way related, then it is more than possible," Tory replied, "All the birds there died off suddenly, and that was the end of it, or so we thought."

"So you think this has been circulating for over fifty years from one bird to the next?" asked Chris.

"That doesn't make sense," she said, "It would have shown up before this and probably in an epidemic similar to what we see now."

"Wait a second, you think this is reaching epidemic proportions?" he asked alarmed by her comment.

"It is entirely possible that this is on the verge. Look at the numerous attacks, and now we have birds and people dying off," she said sadly, "And I don't think this is nearly over."

Lt. Ferguson was returning across the sand and admonished Tory, "Let's not discuss that too loudly around here. We don't want anyone causing a panic over this. This is tough enough to control as it is. We dodged the bullet with the train incident. We don't need to feed that machine."

"Sorry," nodded Tory, "Guess I was thinking out loud."

The lieutenant squeezed her arm and smiled saying, "Yeah I know, I have to watch my own words often around the public. But, we need to be cautious. If any rumors get going, this could get a whole lot worse, and I won't be the only one waving a gun around here."

Tory smiled back and said, "Got it."

Lt. Ferguson had brought a few bags and more gloves and said they should clean up all the birds to prevent a return of the other birds. So the three of them each filled a bag, and Lt. Ferguson said he would run his to Dr. Bennett and the other two could go to UCSD with the grad students.

Tory rode back with Lt. Ferguson to retrieve her car and then headed back toward the beach to wait on the students and word from Dr. Forrester and Prof. Revere. On her return, she spotted something that almost made her run off the road.

As she drove downhill on one of the streets, she saw a church with a giant cross on its hill. There on the top and sides of the cross, she spied dozens of birds perched along every inch. The sight was unbelievable to her because every single one of these was a bird of prey. She pulled into the parking lot of the church and moved the car toward the cross.

As she drove her car closer, she saw the sight had attracted other tourists as well. The people were at the base of the cross taking pictures with their cameras and phones.

She had never seen so many hawks together in one place. Not even at the Wild Animal Park, where they not only exhibited but had a show featuring birds of prey. There were red-tailed, sharp-shinned, Cooper's and Swainson's hawks, a Northern harrier, a white-tailed kite, a couple of ospreys, an American kestrel, and even a peregrine falcon, all jockeying for firm footing on the cross.

"About the only bird missing is the turkey vulture," she said to herself aloud. She looked into the sky and thought maybe she found the vultures but gasped when she realized she was looking at two magnificent golden eagles circling over the crowded perch below.

The people were making lots of noise and were excited at the scene, but they did not seem to disturb the flock of birds. The birds just seemed to stare at the crowd looking as if they were grocery shopping at the growing group below.

They all had a single thought in their heads as they stared at the persons below them, Gotta Eat!

Tory realized too late what was about the happen. She began to shout to the people while moving away from her car. With a sudden flourish of wings, all the birds took flight in unison. They swept down on the onlookers. Tory watched as the birds chose their targets, and began using their effective arsenal of weapons on the hapless group of spectators.

In moments, there were at least two or three birds on

each person, and they were ripping and piercing the individuals. The screams were deafening but ineffective against the barrage.

She ran back to her car as she watched the eagles swoop down at her. She had just got behind the door when the first eagle hit her car window with a heavy thump. Thankfully she had been running the air conditioning coming from the station, as she saw the talons hit the closed window. She started the Jeep and pulled the car closer to the crowd. She laid on her horn steadily trying to scare the winged attackers off their prey.

It was to no avail, and instead, she attracted the attention of a few more birds who were trying to get to her behind the windshield. She looked over to see one fallen woman with two hawks ripping pieces of flesh from her neck and arms. Blood began spurting every direction, and the birds were crazed in their frenzy of meat.

Others were fighting to get the birds off. But like the woman, blood was everywhere, and many could not reach or even see their persecutors.

The birds firmly dug into their backs and faces. The horrifying sight was taking place all around Tory's Jeep and left her feeling helpless as she could only witness the carnage before her.

She grabbed her cell phone and quickly punched 9-1-1 and was yelling into the phone about the attack as the lady at the other end said "9-1-1 Emergency."

It took longer than it should have to convince the

woman at the other end that this was not a prank call, and that in fact people were being killed by birds of prey. Even then, Tory doubted that the woman had the real sense of urgency as she should have in alerting the sheriff's deputies. It did not help that Tory never paid attention to the name of the church or even knew the street she had been on when she entered the lot.

The operator told Tory that she would contact Animal Control, to which Tory screamed at the woman, "We need the sheriff's deputies," and quickly hung up and called Lt. Ferguson instead.

He picked up on the third ring just as Tory frantically thought he wasn't there. She began yelling and crying at the same time, and Lt. Ferguson did his best to calm her down. He knew what church had the giant cross on the hill and told her that he would have sheriff's deputies there in a moment, and he was on his way from the morgue as well.

By the time the first squad car had pulled up, a few of the birds had flown off having gorged themselves from their victims. The sheriff's deputy got out and couldn't believe what he saw. People were strewn all over the parking lot, and field and most still had birds tearing at them. He was trying to figure which birds were doing the worst damage. When he hesitated, Tory rolled down her window a crack and yelled for the sheriff's deputy to start shooting.

He moved to the bird closest to him that had been sitting on a young man's shoulder with a large chunk of meat hanging from its mouth. The deputy fired and sent the eagle sprawling into the field. He then turned to a second person lying just beyond where the shot bird landed and fired again.

From her vantage point in the car, Tory could not see what the officer did, but saw a spray of feathers rise after the gunshot. A second siren was followed by a vehicle with its lights flashing, and two officers flew out of the car, immediately drawing their guns. Whether they had heard the other shots or were better forewarned, they began searching out other victims. The girl that Tory had seen earlier still had a Sharp-shinned hawk on her, and the sheriff's deputy kicked it off her and then shot the bird blowing it's head clean off it's body.

His partner had moved into the field, and after a moment another shot rang out. Right after that Lt. Ferguson's car pulled into the parking lot with its lights flashing and Lt. Ferguson ran to Tory's car and opened the door. Tory fell into his arms and started weeping.

He held her until her sobs slowed and she got under control once more.

"Are you all right? Did you get hurt or pecked?" he asked her.

She shook her head and said she was okay and then said, "I couldn't help them. The birds were everywhere and killing these people, and I couldn't do anything about it. I have never seen anything like this!" And she began crying again.

"You got us here," he told her, "That was the best thing you could have done."

The first of three medical transports arrived and the medics began administering to the survivors. Out of the twelve people that were taking pictures, four were dead, two more died on the way to the hospital, and the other six were seriously injured.

Seven birds were shot and killed. But the rest flew off, either before the police arrived, or soon after the shooting began. Tory guessed there had been about two dozen birds before the attack commenced. That meant more than two-thirds of the infected birds escaped, including one of the two eagles.

"Why only birds of prey?" asked Lt. Ferguson, "We have seen all types of species band together since this started, not just one variety."

"Perhaps they knew they could do more damage together?" Tory said, admitting that was only a guess at best.

"I'll need you to come back to the station with me and tell me everything just as it happened," Lt. Ferguson said almost as an apology.

"That's fine," said Tory, "May I call Chris and Dr. Forrester first?"

"I wish you would," said Lt. Ferguson, "See if Dr. Forrester has any take on why birds of prey would gather like this, and whether he thinks it will happen again."

Tory nodded and walked away to make the calls. After finally convincing Chris that she was all right and did not get a scratch, she called Dr. Forrester.

"I am on my way to the airport to pick up Prof.

Revere, Tory, what's up?" he answered.

She relayed the incident and then asked Lt.
Ferguson's question about why several different species
of the same type would group the way they did, and
what the odds of this event repeating might be.

"I can't imagine. Just as we have seen many species
group during these events, all I can think of is what you
just said, that they know they can be more aggressive if
they flock together. And if that's the case, then yeah,
they could do it again," Dr. Forrester told her.

"Well what I witnessed was nothing short of a
hunting party!" exclaimed Tory, "They just sat and
waited until enough people converged to mount their
onslaught. They stared at the gathering crowd and then
'Bang' they flew into action." Her tears began welling
up again remembering the attack.

"An interesting observation," said Dr. Forrester,
"That may have just been it. Perhaps they are learning
to hunt together. We have seen that every bird examined
thus far has gorged itself of food. Everything in its
stomach and intestines indicate that they have
constantly foraged for meat."

"And not only are they're finding it, they are not
wasting time waiting for it to die first," she said
disgustedly, "I know rabies will make its victims
extremely aggressive, but the savagery I witnessed was
nothing short of a shark-like feeding frenzy."

"I am thankful that you only witnessed it and were
not one of the wounded or worse," said Dr. Forrester.

"Yeah, well I don't think I want to see that side of an

eagle talon again anytime soon," she said with a heavy sigh.

"We will be there in a few hours if Prof. Revere's flight is on time. In the meantime keep watching those skies and stay safe Tory," said Dr. Forrester.

"Not to worry, I will," she answered. After she hung up from Forrester, she relayed her conversation and told Lt. Ferguson she would follow him to the station for his report.

Tory spent the couple hours at the station with the lieutenant filling out reports. Lt. Ferguson could see Tory was still rattled from her experience so he talked in generalities to help calm her. As a result, each learned a little about each others private lives. Lt. Ferguson divorced for many years now, and his ex-wife living in Santa Barbara taught at a junior college. He said she couldn't handle the long hours and high stress of his police work, but they remained friends and occasionally spoke, mostly during the holidays.

Lt. Ferguson got Tory to open up about her eastern Tennessee roots and her love of birds. He was beginning to like Tory as a person, and hoped the trauma she experienced would not leave any permanent scars on her psyche.

When Tory finally finished with Lt. Ferguson she felt a little better about her ordeal. She jumped into her Jeep and went down to meet up with Chris until Dr. Forrester and Prof. Revere arrived in San Clemente.

Later that day, Dr. Forrester and Prof. Revere had followed Tory to the church to gather what remained of the birds involved. Afterward, they met up with Chris after he completed his shift, and the four of them went to a bar that he recommended.

Again, while Tory wished the circumstances were different, she was thrilled for an opportunity to meet and talk with the foremost ornithologist in the field and classroom today. Even Dr. Forrester had to bow to what Prof. Revere had accomplished at Cornell. And here she was asking Tory her opinions in all this.

Prof. Revere was impressed by Tory and her understanding of the behavioral patterns of the birds that she was studying. The various species Tory forced herself into observing was insightful and well-documented. She exhibited an unbridled passion in her theories and hypotheses, and Prof. Revere didn't dispute them. Dr. Forrester just beamed at his favorite student and knew what Prof. Revere was thinking about her. He had felt it a time or two, himself.

The other three involved Chris as much as they could in their discussions, especially when they turned to how this all began. Some of their arguments went over Chris' head, but he was proud to know that the woman he now considered as his girlfriend was attracting so much notoriety from her advanced colleagues. She was doing fine it seemed from their conversations, and no one would have guessed from their interaction that she was any less of an authority than the other two.

After Prof. Revere had grilled as much information from Tory as she thought relevant, she pulled a file out of her briefcase. She said to Dr. Forrester, "I am going to apologize for this even before I show it to you. I understand you hold little stock in this, but I needed to see if there was any relationship between these two incidents, and how it ended before."

This had Dr. Forrester's curiosity up and Tory just smiled and said, "Dare I hazard a guess?"

Prof. Revere smiled and said, "Be my guest."

"Bodega Bay." Tory shot back.

Prof. Revere nodded and said, "I have always obsessed over this event, and this is all the information I have been able to ascertain from everywhere I could pull it. I think there are some distinct similarities."

"I always said that was more of an urban legend, but if you have new information, my mind is open to review it," said Dr. Forrester.

"Atta boy, Bill," Prof. Revere teased him, "After all they had no idea birds had caused the Spanish Flu until many years after it killed around 50 to 100 million people."

"Wait, what?" asked an astonished Chris, "What are you referring to?"

"The Spanish Flu was a pandemic that infected an estimated 500 million people and killed around five percent of the entire world's population in 1918. It was determined many years after the pandemic, that the cause of the flu was a significant precursor virus harbored in birds. Pigs kept near the front during World War I mutated the strain, and subsequently infected humans," explained Prof. Revere.

"My point to that," Prof. Revere continued to Dr.

Forrester, "Is that what if this disease actually existed back in the 1950's but mysteriously died out or didn't spread for some reason? We need to know if that happened and how it stopped before another pandemic begins similarly to the Spanish Flu."

Tory jumped in, "You know this has already killed many people, Andy, at least one girl and one boy from the high school, the young girl Chris helped, three people on a fishing boat, and six from the church. And possibly more people that we don't know about, or others that may be infected by the rabies virus."

"Think of all the people that were injured on that train and probably infected from San Juan. Hopefully, they are getting proper treatment already," added Chris.

"Precisely," said Prof. Revere, "Now, unfortunately, there weren't many survivors from Bodega Bay after the problem appeared and then mysteriously died off after a few weeks. One of the things I was able to discover was that this all started when two lovebirds were brought down from San Francisco. That seems to be when all the subsequent events took place in the Bay. The lady who brought the birds, and the people she was staying with at the time, all passed away shortly afterward. A lot of what is in this file is conjuncture and rumor, but they all spoke of the various attacks."

"There seems to be a major difference here," said Dr. Forrester combing through the file.

"Yes, every attack seems to be made up of the same species," said Prof. Revere.

"No cross-species or flocking together?" asked Tory.

Prof. Revere shook her head, pointed to the reports, and said, "Not according to the records here. This was done by gulls, this one by crows, this sparrows; I find that particularly interesting, read how they found the corpse and what they did to it."

"Wow." said Dr. Forrester, "They certainly did a number on this farmer. Imagine a little sparrow being as vicious as the crows were. There must have been hundreds to do this much damage."

"No birds of prey?" asked Chris.

"No, none. Not even a mention of anything more than a handful of species," answered Tory, "It makes me wonder if we are now dealing with a mutated or stronger strain than the one here. Assuming it is in any way similar, which I guess is a leap."

"Maybe not such a big one," said Dr. Forrester. "Look at the death records that followed shortly after the incident. Many people died that whole year following and mostly due to the flu or respiratory symptoms."

"Rabies!" exclaimed Tory too loudly. She controlled her voice, apologized and said in a lower tone, "That's what they think rabies looks like in the early stages, because of the flu-like symptoms. Then later due to the onset of encephalitis, it destroys the respiratory system."

"Correct," said Prof. Revere, "When we saw we were looking at a new form of rabies in the San Clemente case, I pulled the file and reexamined Bodega Bay."

"What concerns me is if they lost that many people

from just sparrows, crows and gulls, what could we be facing with these bigger birds being affected?" asked Chris.

"I can tell you, I don't want to go through that horrible scene from today ever again," said Tory, "I know I am already going to have nightmares about it tonight."

Chris wished he could comfort her if she had one, and hoped he might soon. He was falling hard for Tory and had been contemplating his life together with hers. But this wasn't the time or place, and he shook himself back to the matter at hand.

"How did this thing end?" he asked when his mind returned to the subject.

"As mysteriously as when it started," answered Prof. Revere, "About two weeks plus a couple of days all the birds began to drop dead. They said thousands were laying everywhere. An ornithologist who was there at the time begged the town to let her do a study of the carcasses, but the sheriff and mayor insisted that all the birds be burned to prevent the spread of any possible disease or to have it affect other birds. Thus, to this day we have no idea what may have been the actual cause, or if that virus died with those birds."

"Maybe what I saw this morning on the beach was the beginning of the same fate," said Chris, "Perhaps this thing will die off as quickly as it started. It has been almost two weeks since Andy first came to me about his attack," A shot of guilt and remorse went through Chris as he remembered Andy.

"There seems to be a few differences in this case," said Prof. Revere.

"Yes, for one the multiple types and cross-species cooperating and foraging together," said Dr. Forrester, "Did they ever say what happened to the lovebirds that started this?"

"No," answered Prof. Revere, "Nothing mentioned after the initial report of the lady bringing them from San Francisco. And the fact that everyone associated with them died soon after didn't help."

"Do we know if any other lovebirds, or for that matter any birds at all, were sold by that same pet store or if anything happened in any other town similar to this?" asked Dr. Forrester.

"I have students researching that very question," she said, "So far they have been unable to find out. Especially as the pet store closed some 15 years ago."

"Well I'm sure that lead went cold a long time ago," Dr. Forrester sighed, "We may never see the connection between there and here."

"I think it is a good guess that whatever caused Bodega Bay long since died off before it got to San Clemente," said Tory, "I still can't picture a bird flying all over California and not infecting other birds before now."

"What if that bird was in isolation?" asked Chris.

"I don't follow," said Prof. Revere.

Chris paused to gather his thoughts and then said to Tory, "You told me there are many domestic birds living decades in people's homes. What if this bird was a pet that somehow escaped recently? Maybe it has carried the virus all its life, but never interacted with other birds until now?"

"Hey, that's not bad, Chris," said Dr. Forrester who was piecing it together, "It would explain why it never showed up between that time and this. And this carrier may even have infected the lovebirds before they left San Francisco for Bodega Bay."

"Great," said Tory, "Now all we have to do is find who may have lost a bird throughout Orange County that may or may not still be alive."

"Well it wouldn't be just any bird," said Prof. Revere, "It would have to be a Psittacoidea, a Cacatuoidea or a Strigopoidea. They are the ones with the longest lifespans in captivity. An Agapornis or Melopsittacus wouldn't live long enough."

"I'm sorry Prof. Revere, but I don't understand anything you are saying," said Chris.

"Sorry Chris, it would have to be a true parrot, cockatoo or Macaw, versus a lovebird or parakeet to live so long, and those type of birds are rarely lost without a reward or notification," she said.

"Well that would narrow the search, but I don't get why we need just that one bird?" asked Chris.

"If it's the carrier of the original virus, we can come up with a proper antidote faster and contain the spread of the virus," answered Dr. Forrester.

"Can't we just use the rabies vaccinations we have now?" asked Chris,

"It may or may not be useful, and we may have a

hard time stopping the spread of the disease among the other birds or people without a possible vaccine derived from the pathogen spread.

Also, since birds carry a higher body temperature, they may have developed a more virulent and resistant strain of the virus then we can treat adequately right now," finished Prof. Revere.

"True," added Dr. Forrester, "We have already seen how much faster this virus works in comparison to the more known form of rabies. We can assume it is as deadly."

"And much more easily spread since it is carried by, and between, birds," added Tory.

"No offense, but you three don't give me much confidence, or hope," said Chris.

"This is no small task, but I know we will be able to enlist the help of the CDC and other agencies as we need them. I am expecting a call from them anytime," said Prof. Revere.

Chapter 10 - Day 16

Dr. Dorsey had his proof on Tuesday morning, but better than that, Dr. James Bennett had already contacted his urgent care facility with information corroborating what he previously expected. The two doctors spoke of the problems, and he admitted to Bennett that he, too, dismissed the bird angle at first and thought there must have been another cause.

"To be honest Jerry," Dr. Bennett confided in the doctor, "I had a morgue full of victims staring me in the face and couldn't see the connection."

"From the disease?" asked Dr. Dorsey.

"No, only one could be tied back to the rabies part," Dr. Bennett said, "The physical attacks caused the rest. These things have become quite vicious in their infected minds."

Dr. Bennett had studied the new virus and determined that while it was possibly airborne, it had a short life outside the host and had to be nearby to spread. This hypothesis could explain why so many birds were infected. It took an infected bird to come into contact with a person and break the skin of that person and to transmit the disease without saliva or other moisture involved.

They had arrived at the same conclusion at both, University of California San Diego, and Cornell

University. They concluded that no moisture needed to be used to transmit the pathogen. It also generated from sources of infection such as the bodily excretions of an infected bird, or where such excrement could accumulate as in lofts, nests, statuary and the like.

Such infected areas could also stay suspended in air currents long enough to travel a short distance, although the rate of infection decreased sharply with any distance between the source and the organism infected.

It was in this way, even more than sharing food, or direct contact, they suspected that the disease was spreading faster. The infected birds were ingesting vast amounts of food. This intake resulted in excreting large quantities of waste material. Contact with, or breathing the "dust" of such excrement after drying, could cause the virus to spread amongst the bird population. Further, this was a stronger virus than the original rabies strain they tested.

In the case of people, apparently, the microbes could survive on the beaks and feathers of the bird for a brief period. Any contact through an open wound allowed the infection to enter the bloodstream and rapidly develop at a highly accelerated rate compared to common mammalian rabies.

There were two bits of good news. It seemed that an infected person would not infect others through respiration or airborne contaminants. It would be several more days and tests to determine how high a risk that proposed. The other was that the disease did not seem to be carried by vectors like flies, mites, or mosquitoes, which pass diseases by biting or stinging humans.

Dr. Bennett had also contacted the National Center for Emerging and Zoonotic Infectious Diseases at the CDC and spoke again with Dr. Lanz. She told him about her conversation with Dr. Dorsey. Now that a second report came in, from a city medical examiner no less, Dr. Lanz was paying closer attention. The fact that apparently, two prominent universities had discovered an entirely new viral form of rabies had now put the entire zoonotic department on high alert.

Notifications went out immediately to neighboring hospitals, urgent care, doctor's offices, and medical associations in Orange County. They warned them about the potential of a new rabies threat from an unusual host, birds. They were to report any patients who had been injured by a bird. The doctors were ordered to be on the lookout for any new or previous wounds from the birds.

The CDC sprung into action. After talking with her boss, the deputy director of infectious diseases, Dr. Lanz got permission to fly a team out of Atlanta to Orange County, Calif. She wanted to get to the bottom of this suspected rabies situation. She ordered the team to conduct a special test of the reported cases. The reference method for diagnosing any suspected cases would be the Fluorescent Antibody Test (FAT), which was recommended by World Health Organization.

Dr. Grant Abernathy headed up the Animal

Resources Biologics Branch and always hoped for a critical case in which he could get involved. Abernathy was in his forties with thick silver hair and a lean build, and he thought he might finally have his wish. So far there were 38 suspected cases with more showing up each day.

Dr. Alice Friedman headed up the Division of Preparedness and Emerging Infections. She outranked Anna Lanz, and was a deputy director, and ran her division reporting directly to the CDC director, himself. She requested to join the team after learning that this might be an entirely new strain with unique properties.

She was only 5-feet-3-inches and had a soft look to her, but everyone knew that Dr. Friedman wasn't someone to get in the way of. Others had tried and regretted their actions later. She obsessed in her pursuit of knowledge. It was her passion to learn everything she could about a new bug. But she was also incredibly organized and structured, which in the panic of a new outbreak, was one of the most important qualities to possess. Since she was the highest ranked, Dr. Friedman would be in charge.

She, Abernathy and several others from various branches were loaded onto a plane from Atlanta. There were employees from the Division of High Consequence Pathogens and Pathology, Rabies Branch due to the potentially fatal nature of the disease, also the Division of Vector-Borne Diseases, the Animal Resources Biological Branch, and others.

This outbreak crossed a lot of borders within the

CDC, and a good many of them had a personal interest in the case. Volunteers were easy to attain, and several got turned away. This outbreak was one of those types of situations that could spotlight a person's career if handled well. Something each of them desired. Everyone getting on that plane felt fortunate to be there, and they had a wealth of talent backing them up from Atlanta.

Of the 38 reported cases reevaluated from their original prognosis to possible rabies infections, three were in a coma, and many more were in advanced stages of the disease. Those begun showing signs of cerebral dysfunction, anxiety, confusion, agitation, and some had also developed delirium, abnormal behavior, hallucinations, and suffered from insomnia and unquenchable hunger.

Except for the hunger, these symptoms were always the final precursor to succumbing to the fatality of the disease and were well past any hope of recovery. No known drug or regimen could save a patient once those symptoms began showing up in earnest. There were less than ten documented cases of human survival from clinical rabies reported, and of those, only two had not had a history of pre- or post-exposure injections.

So the CDC knew that their best hope lied in the cases that were now showing up and hadn't developed beyond a crucial point. When learned that attacking birds had been at the root of this, they watched the feeds from the television stations that had shown the interviews with the numerous victims and the stack of dead birds involved in the attack. Every CDC agent on that plane knew that this would quickly spread.

Especially once learned that those were not isolated attacks. In the briefing, they learned about the birds of prey at the church, the fishing boat, and the high school incidents that took place, along with multiple individual attacks. They could not contain speculation that a potential pandemic was already underway and they were only seeing the beginning of it.

Once they landed they would set up a laboratory and base of operations at the Saddleback Memorial Health Center in San Clemente. Through their vast network of hospitals and medical centers, they were already gathering experts in various fields of communicable diseases to assist the CDC agents upon their arrival.

They were also moving patients suspected of the new rabies virus from the other hospitals and urgent care institutions, to this hospital for testing and treatment. They had currently checked in 30 of the 38 suspected cases and were waiting for the other possibles.

Patients not involved in the attacks were either being released early or moved to other centers in the Memorial community. They needed to make room for the current cases and people expected to be attacked by the birds. Six of those were survivors of what was called the 'birds of prey' event treated for severe lacerations and rabies at the same time.

Some of these victims had experienced extreme nightmares as Tory herself had predicted last night and had to be attended to prevent damaging themselves further. The terror that some of the patients exhibited had worried the staff as to what might be happening throughout their town.

Information was beginning to leak out about the attacks. Through some miracle, they squelched the bird of prey attack from the press. People who were attacked singularly or in groups were suddenly garnering attention from reporters.

Once again, Mayor Turkovitch was threatening editors and producers alike of the consequences of putting her town in a poor light. Many had just ignored her rantings, although the local journalists tried to tread a little lighter to avoid her ire. The ones backing down had their purse strings tied tightly to the town for survival.

She had even tried to convince Dr. Friedman that there was no need for a full-blown assault by the CDC to investigate a couple 'incidents'. After advising the mayor what was what, Turkovitch gave up and figured that she could keep a lid on this through other means.

When contacted by Dr. Friedman advising on what was taking place, Under-sheriff Puerta told Friedman that the man she would want to coordinate with was Lieutenant Joe Ferguson, the Chief of Police in San Clemente. He was heading up the investigation and knew more about these bizarre bird incidents than any other person on the force.

So when Lt. Ferguson got the call from Friedman, he offered to give her a full rundown and volunteered the services of Dr. Forrester, Prof. Revere, Tory, and Chris, as well. He called each of them and told them to expect a phone call and probably a meeting with the CDC deputy soon.

CHAPTER 11 – DAY 17

The next morning, Jean Turkovitch finished up another television interview for the festival that weekend. It was her third so far this week, and she was sure that each one went better than the last. She was also confident this would bring great crowds of people to the Microbrew.

She had "persuaded" a couple of service groups including the Boy Scouts and a church youth group into doing beach clean-ups, and she thought the beach was looking pristine and welcoming in the interviews.

It was time to head back to her office at her home and crack the whip on whoever wasn't pulling their weight for this event. As she walked away from the pier and toward her car, a crow came from nowhere and landed in her hair.

Turkovitch screamed and beat at the bird, almost knocking herself senseless with her purse. The bird flew off and left her with only messed hair, but one would have thought she had been mangled and beaten listening to her.

She saw an approaching officer, who asked her what happened. The stream of obscenities would have made any military lifer take cover as the mayor screamed about the continuous problems with these fucking birds, and why wasn't the sheriff's department doing anything about it?

"Mrs. Mayor, we are doing what we can, but we can't go around with our revolvers drawn shooting at every bird we see," he tried to reason with her.

"If you can't shoot them, then catch them and have them put down," she yelled back. She suddenly realized she was drawing a crowd and that the incident might end up recorded on a video phone or worse. She got hold of her emotions and changed her abruptness.

"Well, I guess it was just a bird that got caught in my hair. The thing was probably confused or didn't see me when it took off," Turkovitch said in a quieter tone, "It startled me is all."

"Yes Ma'am," the deputy agreed. He was perplexed at the sudden change but thankful he wasn't the object of her angst anymore.

She walked off, still fuming on the inside. She had gotten the deputy's name off his badge and would report him for not taking appropriate action later. But for now, she needed to get back and keep the ball rolling on the festival.

In the meantime, Angie Johnson was making sure that sound bites from the previous interviews appeared on the city's web and social media pages. She also had uploaded a radio interview that she did.

Ordinarily, Turkovitch would have done that, too, but it conflicted with one of the television interviews, so she conceded to let Angie do it, with threats that it better be done well or else, of course.

It genuinely seemed that they were getting the most

interest they had ever received for this event. Angie knew now that it would be a huge success. She even had several more vendors begging for a spot for the weekend. She felt terrible that she had to turn them down, but they were jammed to maximum capacity already. With just a few days before the festival, Angie knew this would be the highest crowd of almost any event they ever pulled off.

$$\kappa \stackrel{\kappa}{\kappa} \stackrel{\kappa}{\kappa} \kappa \stackrel{\kappa}{\kappa} \stackrel{\kappa}{\kappa} \kappa \stackrel{\kappa}{\kappa} \stackrel{\kappa}{\kappa} \stackrel{\kappa}{\kappa} \kappa \stackrel{\kappa}{\kappa} \stackrel{\kappa}{\kappa} \kappa \stackrel{\kappa}{\kappa} \stackrel{\kappa}{\kappa} \kappa \stackrel{\kappa}{\kappa} \stackrel{\kappa}{\kappa}$$

By the following day, Friedman and the CDC had taken over the hospital and were in the process of examining and treating the numerous patients. While two people died from the disease the day before, four more came in after being urged by their respective doctors to go to the hospital immediately. That brought the count to 40.

Drs. Friedman and Abernathy met Lt. Ferguson and the others at the conference room at the station. While the seven of them packed the room tightly, Dr. Friedman thought it would be better to discuss this in the sheriff's department than somewhere in public. She honestly had no intention to cause any more of a panic than Jean Turkovitch did from that standpoint.

They ran down the attacks in chronological order, and Lt. Ferguson, Dr. Forrester, Tory, and Chris talked about each incident. Prof. Revere added what she surmised about the cause and spread of the disease from species to species, and what they might expect going forward.

Lt. Ferguson also suggested they visit with Dr. Jim Bennett, the medical examiner, and review the damage that the birds had done to the various victims.

"Our first and foremost concern is to find the host of this disease, if at all possible," said Dr. Friedman, "Although that might be futile at this point, it may assist us in developing a vaccine faster."

"I may have a lead on that," said Prof. Revere, "My students have been working at a fever pitch trying to find which bird may have carried this. They narrowed it down to a purchased Cockatoo from 1963 at a San Francisco pet shop, based on the sales records they were able to get."

"How did they find that?" asked Dr. Forrester, surprised by the new information.

"My students were able to track down a relative of the pet shop, and they still had the sales records in their attic. The City of San Clemente is listed as the buyer of the Cockatoo," she said.

"Then we will need to get the city to tell us what they did with the darn thing," said Chris.

"That may be an interesting problem," said Lt. Ferguson, "The old city council fell to the wayside several years ago, and the current mayor is anything but pleasant, let alone cooperative."

"Indeed," said Dr. Friedman, "She already tried to turn us away and is in major denial that there is anything amiss in her town. But whether she will cooperate or not, we will get the information, even if I need to bring Homeland Security into this. Let them place her in jail for obstruction for a few days."

Lt. Ferguson and Chris couldn't stifle their laughter at the thought of Turkovitch in jail, and both thought that might be a show worth seeing. Lt. Ferguson hoped he'd get the honor personally to escort her to a cell.

"Why would the city buy such a bird in the first place?" asked Tory, "Is it a mascot or something?"

"Not that I ever heard of," answered Chris. Lt. Ferguson just shook his head.

"Whatever the reason, we need to find who has that bird now," said Dr. Abernathy, "I agree with Dr. Friedman that we need to get our hands on it and come up with the right vaccine to treat and possibly halt this disease."

"I am concerned about one thing," said Prof. Revere, "The first known attack was on a homeless man was by a turkey vulture, not a cockatoo,"

"Hmm, you're right," mumbled Dr. Forrester, "Doesn't bode well does it?"

"Am I missing something here?" asked Dr. Friedman, "So what?"

"Well, since the first bird that displayed signs of the disease was a scavenger, it may be possible that the cockatoo had already succumbed to the outside forces and got consumed by the vulture," Dr. Forrester explained.

"So you're telling me we will never find the host?" asked Dr. Friedman.

"It may be unlikely," said Prof. Revere, "Even if

there are remains, it may have been weeks ago, and we can scarcely guess where the vulture's nest was. They throw their nest together haphazardly and will put it anywhere including a cave, outcropping, tree or on the ground."

"Talk about your needle in a haystack!" exclaimed Dr. Abernathy, "I guess we should probably progress without planning on locating the host bird."

"Well I think we need to look anyway," said Dr. Friedman, "It could save us weeks and countless lives if we find it."

"I will make a few calls and get several of my students here to help perform the search," said Dr. Forrester.

"I'll contact the zoological society and see what help I can get as well," said Tory.

"I can have the Sheriff's Department keep an eye out for this. Can you give me a better idea of what we are looking to find? I can't have them hunt for this exclusively," said Lt. Ferguson, "Especially when they are trying to prevent these damn birds from attacking people."

"If the bird that attacked Andy was the first infected, then we should be looking somewhere around there for the nest," commented Chris, "It probably wasn't one of my vultures from San Juan, that would be too far according to Tory."

"Probably not," reasoned Prof. Revere, "However, the voracious appetites of these infected birds might change their foraging patterns as well. But I agree we should start in the immediate San Clemente area and spread out only after that."

"Well why you search for the cockatoo and identify potentially dangerous birds, we will work on containing and curing this disease and coming up with a vaccine, host or no host," said Dr. Friedman.

"I guess we have our marching orders then," said Lt. Ferguson. And with that, he stood and opened the conference room door.

As they began to stand and gather their belongings, Lt. Ferguson asked Dr. Friedman quietly, "Should we be putting out some warnings? People need to be cautious of attacking birds. If they get scratched or cut that person needs to seek medical attention immediately."

"We have already begun getting notices out to the medical community," answered Dr. Friedman, "We are preparing a statement for the public. I will make a public service announcement tomorrow or the day after. We don't want to cause a panic, but we need to let people know there is a real danger out there. We are choosing our words carefully."

"What about those already attacked?" asked Dr. Forrester.

"The CDC in Atlanta is getting the medical records of anyone claiming to have been injured by birds and personally contacting them, including all the train passengers. They are urging they get it checked out at the hospital in San Clemente as soon as possible," answered Dr. Friedman.

Dr. Abernathy added in a low voice, "We don't even

know how easily infected this strain is, so we are looking to treat as many as we can with symptoms first and closely monitor others."

"Isn't that chancy?" asked Chris, "Maybe Andy and others would be alive today if we would have taken action sooner."

Lt. Ferguson turned to Chris and said, "You need to quit blaming yourself for Andy. It was not your fault he died."

"We are doing everything we can to help those injured and possibly at risk," said Dr. Friedman, "And we are not turning away anyone suspected of having rabies. We can only hope that the current vaccines we have can combat this. We probably won't know how effective they are for several days yet."

In fact, already at the hospital, the staff, nurses and doctors were busy administering rabies vaccinations and monitoring vitals and checking for any improvements. People in scrubs and lab coats were moving throughout the various floors at a quick pace. All were trying to administer to anyone they thought wasn't too far gone to be saved.

Under CDC orders, the patients that were the furthest along with the disease were on the ground floor, and for a simple reason. It was closest to the morgue.

The second floor got split in half with the next most severe cases on one side, and those patients who had at least a minimum possibility of recovery at the other wing.

The third floor up was for newly acquired patients

who had only recently begun to show signs of the disease. Their doctors referred most of these. The hope is these folks would recover fully if the right vaccine arrived on time.

Further hope that the current mammalian rabies vaccine would at least arrest the development of the disease. Even if the vaccine could not cure it, as it had done before, it may slow the progress and buy the patients more time.

Everyone in the medical profession knew that beyond a specific development, as was the same as with any rabies infection in the past, nothing could prevent the advancement of the pathogen and it eventually killed the patient.

Those patients were in the half of the hospital that made up the ground and half of the second floor. They were kept as comfortable as possible, and many restrained to prevent them from doing damage to themselves or others.

The staff on the first floor had to wear hazmat suits on the precaution that this might be the most prone to an airborne communication of the disease. While no cases were known to have initiated so far from this threat, there was no need to run the risk of spreading contamination this way now.

They had seen the difference on the slides between the usually known mammalian rabies and the new aviary strain from which these people had suffered. But so far, the host animal had not been located, and so they had nothing in which to prepare a new vaccine that could be more successful. It was apparent to the pathologists that this new strain had mutated at some point. This problem meant it adapted to the physiology of the birds, finding new ways of infecting other hosts.

They also knew that this strain developed much faster and spread more quickly through the body. The team surmised that this virus, because it had mutated in birds that had a higher body temperature than humans, would ravage the body that much faster and spread at a higher rate. They were sub-naming this the Super Aviary Rabies Virus or SARV.

It indeed was not for lack of effort that they had been unable to develop a new vaccine. Dr. Friedman, under the coordination of the CDC, had pooled together microbiologists, epidemiologists, educators, chemists, ecologists, demographers, statisticians, health economists, veterinarians, health communicators, and information technology experts to all work on the problem within hours of her assignment. Nearly everyone in San Clemente that carried any medical degree in the area was asked in some form or fashion, to assist in controlling this problem from becoming an actual pandemic.

From the plane, she had set up infection control centers. And through the use of local health officials, she established a quarantine station that would be on high alert every minute of every day for new victims and attacks.

CHAPTER 12 – DAY 18

Lt. Ferguson had learned from the city's archives and without the need to bother the Mayor's Office that the bird had been purchased as an award and presented to Edward's family many decades ago. He also learned from the family that the bird had died and that something had dug it out of their backyard and carried it off.

He had advised his department about their 'needle in a haystack' mission of finding its remains most likely in or near a vulture's nest. He had a picture of a cockatoo hanging on the wall and was explaining the importance of locating this bird, as a few more suspected rabies cases had already come into the hospital that morning.

"Just imagine if one of your loved ones had been subjected to this disease already," he said to the briefing room full of deputies, "What would you do then to find a cure? I promise that if this doesn't end soon, every one of us will know someone, possibly very close to us, that will have an issue with this."

"Speaking of which, chief," Deputy Collinswood interrupted as he rose his hand. "If we know the birds are responsible for the attacks on that kid, the victims on the boat, church, and high school, what orders do we have if we see these things causing harm while we are out there?"

"That's a damn good question," said Lt. Ferguson, "The problem is we are sequestered under orders from Puerta and the mayor of San Clemente. So we can't say shit even if we have a mouthful. However, the CDC will be getting the word out soon enough. In the meantime, if you see one or more of these things causing harm, as in the church incident, of course, you may use whatever force you deem reasonable and appropriate to save our civilians."

"In other words, blow the goddamn things to hell," yelled out Deputy Jim Schultz in his usual humor. The room erupted in laughter.

"Please be careful not to harm any citizens, or discharge your weapons unnecessarily, or you will have someone else to ride your sorry asses, as it won't be me any longer," warned Lt. Ferguson.

He dismissed the deputies with the reminder to beat any bushes to find the remains of that cockatoo.

ᵏ ᵏᵗᵏ ᵏ ᵏᵗᵏ ᵏ ᵏᵗᵏ ᵏᵗ ᵏ ᵏᵗᵏ ᵏ ᵏᵗᵏ ᵏ ᵏᵗᵏ

Chris went back to work, while Tory, Prof. Revere, and Dr. Forrester all worked on securing and guiding as many volunteers as they possibly could to help find the remains of Sebastian.

Many of Dr. Forrester's students had shown up that same morning to begin searching potential vulture nests and were out trying to locate the vultures through flight patterns and telltale signs of former nests or possible areas of interest to the birds. Only Ashley Galtt and

Dennis Tye, who were at the lab when the news came in, were aware why they were there and what they were explicitly trying to find. Both students, sworn to secrecy as a condition of participating in the hunt, were rewarded by leading two of the group's efforts.

The other students were surprised when they were told 'under no uncertain terms to have any contact with the birds'. At first, they thought Dr. Forrester was kidding them, as even if they were disturbing an active nest, vultures were very skittish and would not want to come anywhere near them.

Prof. Revere explained that these birds might be potentially ill with a new virus they were beginning to document and understand. She told them it made the birds act different than usual, and might show aggression, even a distance away from any nest. They were to exercise extreme caution around any of the local birds of San Clemente or San Juan Capistrano.

They both felt guilty not being able to tell these volunteers more about the disease or warn them of the inherent dangers they might be facing. They did tell them that if any student was scratched or cut by any bird, they were to seek immediate medical attention at Saddleback Hospital and to talk to Dr. Grant Abernathy, and only him.

Even Lt. Joe Ferguson, who seemed unflappable to threats was quite clear that no one talked or said anything more than necessary regarding SARV, or the actions of the birds. He had been against bringing the students up in the first place but admitted to not having sufficient manpower to search the entire area for possible nests.

As it was, the students were having difficulty finding any birds anywhere. They couldn't even scare up any field birds as they trudged around the areas under high tension towers and outcroppings.

The sheriff deputies weren't having any better luck. The birds seemed to have moved off to a new location and were nowhere to be found.

There were very few shorebirds down by the beach as well. Chris had not seen so few seagulls in a very long time. Several pelicans were out amongst the waves as was reasonable, but nothing else. Not even fleet-footed killdeer raced across the sand as they usually did.

Chris thought that perhaps the nightmare that had descended on the South Coast was finally at an end. Just like it had ended in Bodega Bay. After all, it had been over two weeks since Andy had come to Chris and showed him the wound on his side. Everyone said that was how long a span of time it took to kill all the birds up north. Why not the same for here?

He admitted to himself that he would have thought he'd seen more birds wash up on shore than he had. He was also a bit surprised that some birds didn't fall out of the sky around town. He knew there were a great many birds infected. Perhaps they all flew off to a special secret place to die together. He certainly hoped this was precisely the case.

Now if they could conquer the rabies issue at the hospital, everyone could get back to their healthy lives, and he and Tory could get down to making some serious love to each other. He liked Dr. Forrester and Prof. Revere, but they were cramping his love life, and he was becoming impatient.

CHAPTER 13 – DAY 19

It was Friday, and the town of San Clemente was buzzing with excitement for the coming festival. That afternoon would begin the moving-in process as people and companies would start setting up their portable canvas tents and mobile trailers in preparation for Saturday's opening event.

Angie was at her office coordinating with two of the TV studios and a radio station that wanted to do live interviews and a remote broadcast from the pier. She was almost giddy at the attention this celebration was garnering. The weather was holding just as predicted, and she was getting call after call for information for the festival, and pleas for last-minute entries or additions.

Later today she and her assistants would oversee the move-in process and administration of the rules and plans for the Microbrew Festival. She couldn't wait for the crowd tomorrow. The mystery of the birds was already a long forgotten memory.

In fact, if anyone had been paying attention, they might have noticed the eery lack of winged creatures in the skies and branches around the entire region. For the second day in a row, the beaches were devoid of any gulls, and again this morning only a few pelicans floated lazily on the waves.

But everyone was in their private worlds, and nobody

gave it a thought while watching or participating in the bustle of activity that was taking place around the town.

Chris noticed. He had become used to watching the skies for a couple of weeks now. As had been his habit recently on his watch, he kept one eye on the swimmers and one on any birds watching for any signs of trouble or aggression. Both yesterday and today there weren't any birds to watch.

He kept attempting to convince himself they must of all died out. Just like at Bodega Bay, their disease finally killed them. But instead of being relieved, he just knew in his gut that wasn't true. So he became apprehensive wondering about where they might be, and what they might be up to while hiding. The nagging voice in his head that kept reminding him about how the last time the birds had "disappeared." It was the morning of the assault on the train.

He learned that the birds that had washed up on the beach were indeed infected with the rabies virus and due to swelling of the brain they perished. A few more birds had washed up since, but not as many as that day. Every bird was immediately 'bagged and tagged' and sent off for analysis.

Chris knew that there had not been nearly enough birds come ashore on the beach to account for the number of gulls that must have the disease. And listening to Lt. Ferguson's account of the suspected attack on the boat, hundreds of gulls from that event alone were still unaccounted for and not seen.

Chris was not alone in his concern. The three aviary experts were making similar observations. They had met again that morning at a coffee shop to try and map out some areas in hopes of finding what nesting areas the vultures were using. They had received information from the local birder communities after enlisting their help as well. This group had given the trio some known vulture hangouts.

But their discussion was now centered around the lack of birds in the area. "I don't even see any songbirds," commented Tory.

"I have been keeping this to myself, as I thought this was stepping into the twilight zone, but what if these birds are communicating with each other and are coordinating their attacks?" asked Dr. Forrester.

"Well thank goodness one of us brought this up," said Prof. Revere with a large sigh, "Ever since the church incident Tory witnessed, I have given this a lot of thought and I have been wondering the same thing. After all, despite the comments of being 'birdbrained' and the like, we know how intelligent birds genuinely are. Percentage wise they have more brain mass than dogs, and are capable of complex problem-solving."

Tory said, "It would explain why various species are flocking together and joining in with birds they might normally fear. But what about when the gulls attacked the pelican? Wouldn't they attack other birds if driven by their insatiable hunger?"

"Maybe through the malady they share, there is some strange sign or symptom recognized by others with the same disease," said Dr. Forrester.

"Now we are stepping off the edge of reason," said Prof. Revere, she then looked squarely at Dr. Forrester, "And yet I can't help think you are right. When I saw the various species from the train when they arrived, I couldn't believe they were from the same incident, and at first, I thought that you were having some fun with me. Then I couldn't believe that swallows had human flesh in their mouths and stomachs," she continued shaking her head, "Never in documented history, that is except for one other time."

"Yeah," Tory said, "Sparrows from Bodega Bay."

"Precisely," said Prof. Revere.

"So we are hypothesizing that these birds are communicating in some special way with each other?" asked Tory.

"Look how often birds work with other animals, like ravens and wolves, for instance," said Prof. Revere, "We know that ravens will call wolves to penetrate a carcass they find since the raven cannot. We know birds will climb in and clean the teeth of a crocodile. The honeyguide bird will lead a honey badger - and even humans - to a bee's nest to get the honey after it's broken open. Birds lounge on the backs of buffalo, moose, hippos, elephants and zebras picking parasites from them, and they'll even share a residence with ants – their natural prey – and lay eggs that the ants protect from other predators for reasons we can't explain."

"I suppose it would be natural to assume they can make a temporary pact to feed their unquenchable appetites while infected with this disease," said Dr. Forrester.

"How else could they get all the food they think they need?" asked Prof. Revere, "Have you noticed there doesn't seem to be any road kill laying around, or anywhere near here? They are constantly on the hunt."

"Hence the bird of prey attack," said Tory, "And if you are a Mockingbird, how else could you feed on a large mammal like a dog or human?"

"And at this point, we have no idea how many birds could be affected with this," said Dr. Forrester, "If you look at how many species are involved it could be thousands of birds."

"And growing exponentially," finished Prof. Revere.

"Maybe they are already dying off in great numbers somewhere like Chris thinks they might be doing, and that's why we are not seeing any of them," said Tory.

"Do you honestly believe that is what's happening?" asked Dr. Forrester skeptically.

"I guess it's more wishful thinking than believing," answered Tory, "But they have been washing up on shore. So maybe they are dying off in other places."

"It's possible that we are losing some of the early contagions to the disease," said Prof. Revere, "but I'll bet for whatever reasons we will see more birds contracting the disease than dying off for a while, or until we can get a vaccine that will halt the spread of SARV."

"Is that because of the variety of species compared to Bodega Bay?" asked Tory.

"That plus this strain seems more virulent than the one they had there. We already see more assaults here than what was reported there to both individuals and groups," she answered Tory.

"Couldn't that just be because of shoddy record keeping?" asked Dr. Forrester, "After all, they did not allow any investigation or records to help us understand what took place back then."

"True, but whether they were afraid or didn't understand how that might impact the future, we are still left that birds of multiple species are assailing people and animals together," argued Prof. Revere.

Dr. Forrester's students had no luck in searching for the remains of a cockatoo. After he finished his coffee, he said he was going to help Dennis and Ashley in their search today and maybe get lucky himself. He invited Prof. Revere to come along with him.

"Thanks, but I think I would like to stay here and see if I can find where all our feathered friends went to," she answered, "It might give us more insight as to what they might be up to."

"Be careful, look what almost happened to Tory," reminded Dr. Forrester, "We don't need to help them rack up another score and lose one of our top ornithologists."

"Don't concern yourself, I am not going out with a loaf of bread and hoping they'll come feed from my hand," she said sarcastically.

"No they'd ignore the bread and take your hand, along with the rest of you," he quipped back as he stood to leave, "Perhaps you have a point though. It bothers me as well not to see a single bird. Like an errant child, it makes you wonder what kind of mischief they are creating. I'll be looking around, too. Like you, I just don't believe we have seen the last of them. Good luck today, and be careful." He then left for his car.

"If you don't mind, I think I will head off as well," said Prof. Revere to Tory, "Although, I am not even sure where I might begin."

"The problem is they never seem to attack the same location twice," said Tory, "The high school, the train station, a boat, the beach, a church, and of course all the various individual attacks and never repeating. Makes it difficult to know where to begin looking. Would you like me to accompany you?"

"I thought you were going down to see Chris?" Prof. Revere asked.

"It can wait if you'd rather have me help you. I don't want you to drive into a tree while searching the sky," Tory said smiling.

"I wouldn't mind the company and second pair of eyes is always better than one. Besides, I have wanted to talk with you about something," Prof. Revere smiled back at Tory.

"Oh, what's that?"

Prof. Revere looked closely at Tory and said, "You know both Dr. Forrester and I are very proud of you. I hope you realize that while Dr. Forrester sent every one of his students chasing after different projects, he has kept you close to us. You have truly been the apex in this situation. And while I'm at it, I want to add my thanks for getting me involved in this adventure, no matter how it turns out."

Tory just blushed and said, "Thank you, Professor Revere."

Prof. Revere motioned for them to get going and as she approached the car and unlocked it, she said, "I think we should check out the more populated areas around here. Something about the train station and school triggered a thought that says they may be looking for more prey moving locally. Anyway, it's a place to start."

"I don't know if I should wish us luck or hope we don't find a single bird," Tory said as she got in, "In some ways, I don't ever want to see another bird."

"I certainly hope that isn't true, and I further hope that this won't change your major or cause you drop out of the program," said Prof. Revere with concern.

"I guess I'm not ready to throw the towel in at this point," said Tory with a sigh, "But this has rattled me to my core."

Prof. Revere backed the car out of its parking space and pulled onto the main road through town. "I don't think you would be human if it didn't."

"Now what I want to talk with you about is a little tacky, and underhanded to poor Dr. Forrester. But I have been thinking about this since shortly after I got here. I would like to offer you a full ride with me at Cornell to get your doctorate, along with making you my assistant for your duration there."

Tory's heart leaped into her mouth, and all she could respond with was "Excuse me?"

Prof. Revere said conspiratorially, "I hope you don't tell Dr. Forrester just yet, as I know it might crush him, but if you decide, I'd love to have you."

"That's extremely flattering, and I hardly know what to say," Tory dumbfounded by the offer, had never contemplated such a possibility. She said more to herself than Prof. Revere, "I have been quite happy with the program at SDSU, and of course Dr. Forrester has been wonderful to me as well," she then trailed off and bit her lip.

"Well think about it. I promise I won't bring this up again until this whole thing is over, but I hope you will consider making the switch," Prof. Revere said.

Tory's mind was now racing with possibilities. Dr. Forrester had always treated her as an equal and was instrumental in helping her achieve the position at the Zoological Society and her current project with them. But Prof. Ellen Revere was unequaled in her field, and Tory quite probably could write her own ticket if she were to study under her, let alone being her assistant.

But then there was Chris. She was falling hard for him. He was a gentle and compassionate person, and she was anxious to take their relationship to the next level. She was going to ask him soon if he didn't ask himself.

He was acting like she needed to bring him a note from Dr. Forrester and Prof. Revere to say it was all right. She laughed out loud at the thought, and Prof. Revere asked her what was funny?

She explained as one woman to another and decided to test the confidentiality of this new relationship with Prof. Revere. She told Prof. Revere that she understood why Chris was hesitant. She guessed he thought he was continually under their watchful eye.

Now Prof. Revere laughed and said, "I genuinely like Chris. He seems to be grounded and quite smart, although he doesn't seem to have any ambitions for his future just yet. I hadn't thought about that wrinkle when I made my proposal to you. I guess you do have some things to consider."

Tory wondered what things would be like when it finally got to that next level, as she was confident it would. What could she hope for their future together once she announced she was off to the other side of the country for her next term and beyond?

She told Prof. Revere that Chris had already expressed an unwillingness to move from his South Coast beaches for any reason. She wondered out loud how he might feel about a long distance relationship? Then she thought as Prof. Revere's assistant; she wouldn't be able to have extended breaks away from Cornell like most students. That fact could make a long distance relationship next to impossible.

She decided to change the subject and asked Prof. Revere how she got into ornithology.

Prof. Revere chuckled and said, "I was just a young girl in high school when I heard the most bizarre news story. Apparently, there was a little seacoast town assaulted by this flock of birds..."

"You are kidding," Tory exclaimed, "Bodega Bay got you into the study of birds?"

"It was something that piqued my interest, and I thought if birds could mount a coordinated ambush like this, how intelligent might they truly be?" she said, "The rest, as they say, was history."

"No wonder you wanted to come here so quickly," said Tory.

Prof. Revere laughed and said, "I had tried to convince my mom to let me go when I was in high school, but of course she said 'no'. By the time I could finally get there on my own, any information was long lost or buried."

They cruised around in silence for the next twenty minutes searching the skies and trees for any sign of their elusive prey. Tory pulled the phone out of her shorts. She said she was going to check in with Lt. Ferguson to see if he had fared any better. She punched up Lt. Ferguson's number, and when he answered, she would bring him up to date on their discussions.

"I was going to call you in a moment and learn how you were doing?" he answered without even saying hello.

"Since I initiated the call, you get to go first," she teased him.

"Nothing, nada, zip, zilch, a big fat zero. We haven't found anything, heard anything or had any problems reported. It is almost like the world's back to normal," Lt. Ferguson told her.

"Well, we aren't so certain about that here, although

we are trying to piece together what they may be up to." She told him that Dr. Forrester had gone to assist his students with some possible nesting areas and that she and Prof. Revere were trying to find where all the birds were hiding.

"Please do me a favor and don't stop at any churches," he added sarcastically.

"No promises. Like we said earlier, it seems eery that no birds are gathering anyplace we can see. We will report back if we see anything strange." She hung up on him and thought that he might be an excellent person to talk to about her new dilemma.

Tory had lost her parents not long after her high school graduation. Her dad died of a heart attack that autumn, and her mom in a car accident a year later. She liked Lt. Ferguson and knew that he was fond of her as well. She also had seen that he was a patient listener in his own right.

Prof. Revere and Tory traversed the area going back and forth around shopping centers, tourist areas, various beaches and parks, and other places they thought the birds might have gathered. They could scarcely find an errant sparrow. It was as if someone had scooped up every bird in the whole area and carried them off to places unknown.

They covered the whole western part from Capistrano Beach to the southernmost part of San Clemente.

While Prof. Revere and Tory searched far and wide for the birds, it was becoming a desperate situation at the hospital. Three more people had died, and seven more had taken their spots in the critical wing.

The vaccinations had come too late to save many of the people who later died. It was unlikely to avoid losing any of the now 23 people that were in the highly critical areas either. What made matters worse, it seemed that even the ones that hadn't shown advanced stages of the illness were not improving. The vaccine wasn't strong enough to reverse or arrest the development of the rabies cells for very long.

The CDC had laboratories in every part of the country working on finding a cure. This rabies strain was like, and unlike, any other they had seen. It had many similarities to mammalian rabies, but it also ravaged cells at a much faster and more aggressive rate. Apparently, it could infect T-cells faster than the body could build immunities to fend them off.

Rabies vaccinations are a slow inoculation process given over several weeks. This infection spread at a much faster rate than the other, and they could not risk inoculating at quicker than the prescribed dosage.

After the first dose, doctors were not seeing the desired secondary response they needed against the pathogen. Apparently, the vaccine wasn't fighting the antigen cells that infected them as it had in the past. By the time they would be able to deliver the second dose, the disease would have spread, and the vaccine would be ineffective against stopping the progression of the infected cells.

They saw that the vaccinated cells were not responding to the virus with sufficient antibody strength to kill the infection. Doctors talked about how "the antibodies were not binding to the pathogen." The treated cells resulted in 'killer T-cells' not being able to break down and destroy the viral attacks. Plain and simple, the vaccine didn't work.

It did seem to slow the degradation somewhat, but as far as being a cure, it was useless. Everyone in the field placed more pressure finding the host so they could retrieve the original antigens and make a stronger vaccine. They heard rumors and were losing confidence that the host would be found at all, let alone in one piece.

Everything the birds attacked that lived became infected, so far nothing seemed to be immune, which was the only other chance the pathologists had in finding a stronger vaccine. If they could locate an animal that rejected the introduction of the antigen at the onset and duplicate the T-cells from its blood, this might do it. In other words, they had to find an animal naturally immune to the new strain. So far none existed.

ĸ ⼙⼙ ĸ ⼙⼙ ĸ ⼙⼙ ĸ ⼙ ĸ ⼙⼙ ĸ ⼙⼙ ĸ ⼙⼙

San Clemente had a large industrial park that was east of the central part of town. The community was at the doorstep of Camp Pendleton Marine Base, and its

125,000 acres. The industrial park grew out of necessity to service the base with all types of needs, along with the ever-expanding population of the South Coast.

There were many different companies from pharmaceuticals to food additives to magazine publishers scattered throughout the eastern hills. Today there was something additional. On every one of the hundred or so buildings roofs, birds had flocked. They were spread out and chattering amongst each other. Each one was making its distinctive calls. It seemed quite the conversation, with the screeches of hawks mixing with the caws of the crows, screams from gulls and voices of the songbirds.

Some of the workers in the area tried to take pictures of the sight, but the birds were too high up or far away, so the photos weren't exciting or clear enough to post on their computers or social sites. Birds seemed to be winging their way and adding to their numbers from every direction. Through the cacophony of noise, there appeared to be a common purpose...and a plan...forming.

CHAPTER 14 – DAY 20

It was already 72 degrees before the sun broke the horizon. It was a glorious morning that Saturday. When the sun hit the pier, it reflected off more than 100 canvas and metal roofs lining both wooden sides and spilling out onto the fringe of the sandy beach. Hoards of people were setting up for what was sure to be a vast number of customers.

Angie had been at the base of the pier in the Chamber of Commerce's tent well before dawn. She had a few other chamber assistants with her, and each one was trying to help the vendors complete their set up and answer their questions. Many on both sides were used to the madness that always proceeded an event like this, and took it like the veterans they were.

The newer chamber volunteers had almost as many questions as the vendors, but even this didn't bother Angie. She knew this was going to go down as one of the most popular events in the town's history. She already had seen several tourists arriving in an attempt to grab one of the better parking spots closer to the shore, and the first of the local TV stations had pulled in to set up.

She guessed that more than a few of the tourists would be staggering to their car for a nap long before lunch. She had seen this in previous years, and the town was well prepared. The sheriff's department forewarned patrons with signs that there would be deputy sheriffs checking drivers before they pulled out of the parking lot. Those not sober enough to drive would have to make other arrangements to get home. They would either have to find a friend or relative, or take a cab, period.

This occasion was the only event that didn't insist on the overnight parking restrictions that were generally in force during weekends. The city held public safety above inconvenience. The sheriff's department brought in reinforcements, and lots of overtime offered to any who wanted it for this Saturday. Several good stories came out of each Microbrew Festival, and for the most part, it was always harmless fun, so many took the opportunity to sign on.

Lt. Ferguson even felt relaxed about this weekend. Ferguson was in charge of making sure the event went off without a hitch. He hoped all these people might scare the birds away for the whole time. And if you have all your rotten apples in one barrel, they are easier to guard than when scattered all over the place.

As 10 am approached everyone was in their places. The mayor of San Clemente greeted the growing crowd. She welcomed them on a portable stage to this year's Microbrew Festival and invited them to enjoy all her town had to offer. Turkovitch wasn't about to waste a large crowd and was politicking to her heart's content about all the strides she had made possible at San Clemente.

After a short while, she realized that the crowd had moved past her and onto the pier. The mayor finally brought her remarks to a close. There was some polite applause, mostly from those that lived and worked in San Clemente. The rest of the crowd pushed past the makeshift stage that promised to hold more exciting entertainment a little later.

Chris had always arranged to take this weekend off, as he enjoyed the festival as much as anyone, and this was one of those times he preferred the role of tourist to being their protector. He invited Tory to join him for the event. One perk was that he was allowed to park at the lifeguard station and avoid having to show up at dawn or park a couple of miles away like so many others.

Tory welcomed the diversion and thought that maybe a couple of beers might give her a clarity that so far her sober mind had not provided. Even Dr. Forrester and Prof. Revere were going to join in the festivities later. Dr. Forrester's wife was coming up to be with him, and they all would hook up with Prof. Revere later that evening for dinner.

Prof. Revere had said she saw enough beer bashes like this at Cornell and wasn't up for a "local version of a frat party", as she called it. But she was all for having dinner together and meeting Dr. Forrester's wife.

Tory decided to wait until the immediate problem with the birds was over before making a decision regarding Cornell. Perhaps by then, a brilliant solution would present itself. And if not a solution per se, at least a resolve in her mind about which path she needed to take. In her mind, there was no sense changing the situation until required. At least, that is what she told herself. Besides she had other more important plans with Chris for tonight.

When they arrived at the beach, they were both amazed at the number of people already in attendance. Chris said that he never saw such a crowd at the event this early before.

"They must be giving away the beer this year," he said chuckling. "I can't even imagine what this crowd is going to look like by noon."

"I am ready to mingle and bump elbows with those of my kind today," Tory said smiling, "Just like Prof. Revere said, it reminds me of some of the parties I was at when I was a newbie at college. That was before I realized that the liquor was never going to run out, and I could take more time to enjoy it."

"Oh, so now the secret comes out that you were a party girl in college. So there is a wild side to you," Chris was happily surprised to learn this.

"I almost overdid it my first year," she said reminiscing, "I learned in my second year to slow it down and take it easy. I was getting over losing both my parents that freshman year and had a destructive streak in me. Luckily I hooked up with my best friend the beginning of my second year before I completely lost my scholarships."

"Again I am sorry about your parents. But I don't think you are going to lose anything today," said Chris and then a thought crossed his mind, "Unless you are worried about your professors being here later?"

"Not today," she said with a laugh, "I am living for

the moment and the day. Besides, I have my lifeguard if I get into trouble." and she squeezed Chris' arm tightly.

They moved to the Chamber tent, and Chris called to Angie. She turned at the sound of her name, and a huge smile broke onto her face.

"Well, Mr. Palmer, it's about time you showed your face!" she yelled above the crowd, She went over, and the two hugged each other. Chris introduced Angie as his friend. He told her that it was Angie who helped him get into the lifeguard program, and is mainly responsible for getting him moved to this area.

"He grew up next door to me in the valley," explained Angie, "I got smart and moved down here while Chris was still in high school, and I told him to come look me up when he got out. He waited six more years before he finally found me." Angie punched him in the arm for emphasis, "But he finally did and as a paramedic no less."

"This looks incredible," Chris said changing the subject, "I think this will be your biggest turnout ever."

Angie beamed, "Yeah, I think we pulled it off this time. I expect 7,500 this year which would shatter all previous festivals. We've been fortunate."

"I'll bet fortune had less to do with it than your hard work," said Chris.

"Well a little of both, anyway." she said.

"So how about letting me get some tickets for Tory and me?" he said getting to the matter at hand.

Angie got behind the table and picked up the roll of tickets. She unrolled a dozen tickets and tore them from the roll. She handed them to Chris, and he attempted to give her a $20 bill.

She waved it off and said to him conspiratorially, "Now you know better than that. When have I ever charged a lifeguard for this? You guys work very hard and keep all our visitors, and us residents, safe. I won't take your money."

Another hand reached out and grabbed the bill from his hand. "Well that's a nice sentiment, but it doesn't pay the bills," said Jean Turkovitch, "12 tickets is $12." Turkovitch fumbled in the box and returned $8 to Chris saying, "Thank you for supporting San Clemente." Then she moved to another person in line.

Dumbfounded and red-faced, Angie just stood there and then turned and apologized to Chris.

"Don't give it a thought," shrugged off Chris, "She's right, this is for a good cause, and I am happy to do my part. I'll catch up with you when you aren't so crazy, and we'll have a beer together." He took Tory's hand, and the two moved onto the pier.

"That's some mayor you guys have down here," said Tory, "I'd bet she doesn't have a decent bone in her body."

"Many would agree with you," replied Chris, "Most say that if she hadn't bought her way into office, that she wouldn't have been worthy of a street sweeper's position."

"I think that's an insult to street sweepers," she said. She then remembered that today was going to be a good day and she abruptly changed her attitude and said to

Chris in a bubbly tone, "So what should we try first?"

"There is a brew from Long Beach that I have started out with first for the last few years. I always like to get that one first because it is a mellow but flavorful brew, which helps my palate get in the right frame of mind for the rest."

"Spoken like a true connoisseur!" said Tory. "So where is this starting brewery?"

Chris pointed to a tent almost halfway down the pier, "Right over there." They began making their way to the station.

Once more Chris was amazed as they made their way through the crowd. He remembered last year he almost walked right to the tent without any interference, and this year he had to jockey around a good many people to get to his destination so early.

When they got to the tent, he asked for two blond ales and passed the first to Tory. She tasted it and exclaimed, "Oh, that's especially good! I may hang here for the day."

"What? And miss all the other wonderful flavors around here? Not with me as your escort," admonished Chris. "We'll finish up here if you still feel that way later, but for now we have many more breweries to test."

The sheriff's department was also surprised by the number that was pouring into the parking lots. Already the first lot was filled and had been cordoned off. The second was filling fast with an unbroken line of cars coming off the main street and no end in sight. This event was going to be rougher than they thought. And they knew once the temperature got hotter, the tempers of people trying to get to the beach would rise to match.

Sgt. Chuck Crowe was already trying to figure out where he would send cars after the parking lots were full. He had done numerous festivals, and while he didn't mind the overtime today, parking duty was his least favorite job as a peacekeeper.

Chuck was in his forties and weighed a solidly built 220 pounds. He was starting to gray at the temples, and he was already looking forward to his retirement in two more years. He wasn't the most congenial member on the force, but he was a good man to have at any event because he brought his balance of strength and persuasion.

He told one of his younger officers to take another cop and begin diverting the traffic to the parking lots behind the main street shops. "And don't let them mess up all the other cars trying to get to this, or you will have a real problem on your hands."

The younger officer nodded and tapped another officer, and they walked off up the street. They were both happy to get away from what they guessed would be a more significant problem very shortly.

In spite of having to work next to the person Angie liked least in all of San Clemente, she was enjoying herself and was basking in the success of the festival. They were selling tickets like crazy and had already gone through two full rolls, and it wasn't even 11 in the morning. The sun was heating up and soon it would hit the 83-degree forecast. That could only help sell more tickets.

She could see the sidewalks full of new arrivals and knew all her efforts paid off. Nothing was going to ruin this day, and even Turkovitch would have to eat crow today, or at least admit it was a raging success. Angie knew of course that the mayor would take all the credit, but at least Angie knew her position would be safe again for the time being.

There was even a lovely breeze flowing in from the ocean, and she looked up to see the palm trees swaying. That's when her heart sank.

Crows filled the tops of the trees. She watched as more came to join them. A few each time, but their numbers were growing steadily. She looked over to the roofs of the buildings across the street, and there were more and different varieties of birds. The pigeons she was used to seeing, but the jays, mockingbirds and smaller birds that gathered with them was unusual. She looked high into the sky and saw there were birds circling. Vultures and hawks were lazily gliding on the currents and were little more than dots high in the air, but Angie saw that more were joining the group and that it was getting more dense with every passing moment.

Angie would have been even more alarmed if she could have seen the ocean behind her. They set the Chamber's booth in front of a restaurant, so her view was blocked by the building.

No one else seemed to notice the growing number of

seagulls that were meeting up about a quarter mile off the pier, and just floating on the waves.

Thirty or more surfers were lining both sides of the pier. The wave riders were a common occurrence on the weekends. The sight of the gulls sharing the waves was typical, and the surfers thought nothing of it. Although if you had asked them, they would have commented that there seemed to be more than usual and their numbers were still building.

Tory felt a tap on her shoulder and spun around to see Dr. Forrester and another woman standing behind him. She said hello, and Dr. Forrester introduced his wife, Natalie. She shook hands with Tory, and then Chris, saying, "So you two are the ones my husband goes on incessantly about every day. Well, it is finally nice to meet the both of you."

Natalie was a charming lady in her late forties if Tory was guessing correctly. She wore her brunette shoulder length hair in a bob and curled under slightly. She was an attractive woman and was dressed smartly in a powder blue blouse and floral skirt ending just above the knees.

They both had a cup in their hands. Dr. Forrester said they began at the base of the pier at the first brewer they came to that had beer. Chris convinced them that this was a much better stop and they agreed to get their second tasting there.

After Dr. Forrester and Natalie had their cups, Chris and Tory took them to another of Chris' favorites toward the end of the pier. He was trying to lead them away from the swell of the crowd that was now bottle-necking the base of the dock.

Chris again commented that he had never seen so many people at this or any event he could remember in San Clemente. He stopped at the brewery and got a cup of darker liquid from this brewer. Tory was staying with the lighter brews for the time being. She said it was good, but not as good as her first tasting.

Dr. Forrester was explaining to Chris why there was such a vast crowd, "Well I think it is the combination of the beautiful sun, the ideal temperature, and the gorgeous ocean..." Dr. Forrester was using his hand and arm to convey with a flourish all he was saying, and he stopped in mid-speech as he turned to include the ocean.

It looked like flotsam on the water. It was hard to tell the mass were birds. The group was tightly packed, and floating wingtip to wingtip and beak to tail. All four stopped and stared. Tory dropped her cup splashing beer on her and Chris.

"Um, I believe we might have a problem here," Chris said quietly aloud not taking his eyes off the sight or even acknowledging the spilled beer.

"You can't honestly believe they would try to attack with all these people?" asked Tory rhetorically.

Dr. Forrester looked up into the sky and quietly said, "Shit."

The other three looked up, and Natalie Forrester gasped. The vultures and hawks were still very high up, but now it looked like a giant cloud hovering directly above them. It was such an enormous group; they looked like they should have numerous mid-air collisions from the sheer number of birds.

"What the hell can we do? We can't start yelling that birds are going to attack, we could either cause a panic or get laughed right off the pier," said Chris.

"Tory, I believe you should call Lt. Ferguson," Dr. Forrester said as calmly as he could, "I would at least alert him to what we are seeing."

Since they were at the other end of the pier, the four of them were too far away to see the buildings and trees that were now completely covered with winged creatures. A couple of people at that end were complaining having received a dousing of excrement from the crows in the trees. As there were so many people and birds together, it was almost impossible to miss getting droppings on every one.

Angie was trying to tell Turkovitch that they might have a situation, but the mayor almost bit her head off and announced that a mere mention of those damn birds would be enough to send Angie packing for good.

Angie looked at the crowd then back to the birds. She thought about the train incident. She was doing the same as Chris and company were on the pier, trying to determine if they would attack the crowd, or merely try to pick people off as they moved away. Everyone who noticed the growing mass knew one thing for sure. Every passing moment added more and more birds to the multitude. They were to the point of pushing each other off their perches as they arrived.

Joe Ferguson saw the caller ID and said as he picked

up, "Please tell me you are not under attack again?"

"Not yet, but it seems imminent," said Tory. She gave him the details and told him that while none of them had a clue what to do about it, that he may want to put his deputies on alert and think of a way to peacefully move these thousands of folks out of harm's way.

"Are you telling me you truly believe that these crazed birds are going to descend upon thousands of visitors and start pecking away?" Lt. Ferguson asked in disbelief.

"Dr. Forrester and Chris seem to think so, too" answered Tory as calmly as she could. "Lieutenant there is a cloud, and I mean a massive cloud of birds of prey circling above us. Further, there is an island full of gulls floating not more than a few hundred yards away from us. You have seen what those gulls can do. I don't think they are just taking in the sights, and unless you want the coroner hanging around here today, you may want to try and figure out what to do about this situation."

"Well, the first thing I want you to do is to grab the others and calmly, but not slowly, get off that damn pier. You are trapped there if you don't. Don't worry about anyone else right now. Don't take time to call or warn anyone. We don't want you to incite a panic."

Lt. Ferguson was thinking as he was talking, "I will call Sgt. Crowe and have him stop letting cars come in and begin turning away pedestrians, but first and foremost, I need you to get to safety. Have Chris get you to the lifeguard office and stay put. I need to go now." And he hung up.

While Tory spoke to Lt. Ferguson, Dr. Forrester called Prof. Revere to warn her away from the area. He only got her voicemail, but he left a frantic message telling her to avoid the beach area at all costs and that he would contact her later. He hung up at the same time as Tory.

Tory relayed Lt. Ferguson's message, and the four began to move as quickly as the crowd would allow them to the back of the pier.

"This isn't going to be easy," said Tory as she held onto Chris tightly.

"We need to keep moving. Stay with me as I do this often in my job," Chris assured her.

Dr. Forrester and his wife were keeping up as best as they could, but apparently, Chris knew better as to how to move through a crowd. Pretty soon there was a fair distance between the two couples, and it was growing.

Tory saw that Dr. Forrester was lagging behind and asked Chris to stop and let them catch up. Chris reluctantly turned and urged Dr. Forrester to keep up. Chris was unmistakably scared about Tory getting caught there when the birds began their charge.

The other couple finally caught up with them, and Tory took her other hand and grabbed Dr. Forrester's free hand, and the four were off once more. As they neared the back of the dock, it became like salmon swimming upstream as the crowd was heading in the opposite direction, and they were going against the continuing flow of people trying to get onto the pier.

A few times Chris called out "Lifeguard coming

through, excuse me, please." But because he was not in uniform, most people just ignored him or occasionally responded, 'Yeah, right.' But he was able to make headway even so.

He had almost reached the base when he saw it. All he could think of was when hunters were trying to flush birds out of the brush. The sheer mass of birds darkened the scene in front of them. As they watched the assemblage raise to the sky, they met the cloud of birds descending from above.

Even though they were further away, they could also see behind them the explosion from the water of gulls joining the ranks. The combination of all the birds joining together gave an incredible sight. It seemed impossible that once a moment ago there was beautiful sunshine, there now existed a pale shade over the entire crowd.

Then the sky fell.

The assault came from everywhere and covered one end of the pier to the other. People covered in birds of every size, description, and voracity. Pigeons were pecking at anything as viciously as were the hawks and vultures. What a moment ago was laughter and good times had melted into a horror of screams.

The carnage was absolute. A few of the stronger men were trying to grab the birds and wring their necks, but even this strategy wasn't effective as there were too many birds pecking at their exposed flesh. They couldn't grab one bird without several more lighting to bite their hands and arms first.

Sgt. Crowe and his force were running down the street toward the pier, and a couple had drawn their guns. But how could they possibly shoot anything without injuring the people as well? It wasn't feasible. A couple of cops pulled their nightsticks, but again they could do more damage to the person trying to beat the birds than attempting to harm the bird itself.

Before the sheriff's deputies made it through the sand to the pier they, too, were being assailed from above. The cops had to fight for their own lives before they could assist anyone else. Sgt. Crowe had been grabbed by a great horned owl at the back of the neck while several jays were trying to peck at his eyes. Strong as he was, he couldn't shake the birds and just kept batting them with his gun drawn. As Sgt. Crowe reached up to strike one of the jays, the owl bit his hand, and his reflexes pulled the trigger. The shot went directly into his head dropping the deputy where he stood.

The tents and temporary shelters were of no value either, and many were toppled from people and things falling into the legs of the coverings. They were going down quickly, and some people tried to hide under the canvases to seek refuge from their attackers.

Chris saw this, and he took Tory to the nearest canvas and began to pull it over them. She yelled for Dr. Forrester to join her and despite protestations from the owners of the tent, soon the four of them were under the canvas, and Chris was once more leading them to the beach area.

The birds tried to get to the group under the moving

tent but couldn't gain purchase on the slick fabric as it moved, and quickly moved to more accessible targets on the pier.

They finally made it to the sand and Chris through a small break in the covering, got his bearings and headed toward the lifeguard station.

On the pier, the chaos was total. Birds and people were so intermingled that one could not tell one from the other. One of the deputies was now about a quarter up the pier, and he still had his gun drawn, while beating away other birds with his hand. He saw a fierce-looking hawk with its wings spread on the rail of the pier. The hawk was looking threateningly at a teenage girl.

The officer aimed at the bird, and just as he pulled the trigger a vulture hit him full on in the face. As he spun, the weapon discharged. The bullet tore through a young man in his twenties and sent him sprawling to the wood planks with a hole in his chest.

The hawk jumped onto the teenager and began what the officer thought it planned to do. The girl's screams mingled with everyone else that was yelling and screaming and was lost in the din. The officer with the vulture was now on the pier and was covered in seagulls along with the vulture and was losing the fight for his life.

The flesh of nearly every attendee was being torn and ripped in every direction and blood was pouring through the slats under the pier and dripping into the ocean. Some people fell off the side of the dock and dropped 30 feet into the water where they were knocked unconscious and drowned.

Some hit the pilings on the way down and were dead even before they hit the water. While a few had taken birds with them, most took wing immediately after the person fell over the rail to find a new victim.

The birds were vehement in their onslaught. They relentlessly went from one person to the next, and after a half hour, nearly every person was laying on the pier trying with the last of their strength to cease the continued slaughter. Some of the birds had gorged themselves and flown off, but too many were still there when reinforcements arrived.

Now the deputies were able to move through the pier and beat or shoot as many birds as they could. The birds realized that it was time to leave and began flying off. A couple of officers brought shotguns and were blowing several birds out of the sky as they tried to make good their escape.

Birds and people floated all around the pylons. The water was littered with bodies and some called out for help. The cries emanating from the pier were horrific. Fathers and mothers sobbing for their children, spouses screaming for their loved ones, friends begging their friends not to be dead. It was as bad as any battle scene from a terrible war.

Angie was under a tarp she had at the back of the tented area, which now lay in shreds before her. She had numerous cuts and was grateful to be alive, unlike the women that lay sprawled in front of her. Angie became sick and vomited at the sight of them.

One, in particular, had lost both eyes and most of her face ripped away from the attack. If it weren't for the outfit that now hung blood-soaked and loosely about her, no one would have recognized Jean Turkovitch as she laid face up and dead in the sand.

The city summoned every ambulance and medical unit from a twenty-five-mile radius. The governor was called and immediately placed the military base on alert and requested all emergency personnel volunteer to assist. Within an hour, there was nothing but the army and emergency vehicles converging within a mile of the beach. They moved the injured further away from the pier. Many received cuts and bruises from falls and running to their cars and other shelters, rather than from the birds.

Armed soldiers were now walking the area with orders to shoot any remaining birds, and that it no longer mattered if they were thought to be rabid or not. All were to be considered dangerous. Some of the birds that got shot could not even be recognized afterward as the bullets exploded their small bodies, and only a few feathers remained.

The remaining birds that could retreat flew away as soon as the first rifle reports sounded.

The worst of the ambush took place on, and near, the pier. The birds knew that this was their best opportunity. That just like trapped animals, this offered the least chance for their prey to escape, and the best hope for doing their worst. Now, the only birds remaining were dead ones.

Chris and the others had made it to the Lifeguard Station and were safe from the decimation. Only Natalie Forrester got cut when one of the birds had managed to grab her hand through the fabric that she desperately clung. She didn't see the type of bird as she was under the tarp.

By some miracle and the quick thinking by Chris, the others were unharmed. Chris immediately pulled out the first aid kit and administered antiseptic to Natalie. He looked at Dr. Forrester with a concerned look, and Dr. Forrester just nodded.

"I'll get her over to the hospital and Dr. Abernathy today," said Dr. Forrester.

Natalie protested and said, "It's a scratch, I'll be fine."

"I'm afraid you will need treatment for rabies," said Dr. Forrester, "We know that even a minor scratch has resulted in some serious illness and my beautiful lady is not going to get sick from this." He held her hand and looked at the cut as Chris applied the bandage.

"My God, how many casualties and injuries do you think there was?" asked Tory looking at the number of ambulances and cars with flashing lights.

"Too many," answered Chris.

"Yes, and there would have been four more if not for your quick thinking, my friend. I can't thank you enough for saving us all," Dr. Forrester said to Chris and patted him on the shoulder.

"I wish I could have saved more and I hope some of

my friends like Angie are okay," he replied to Dr. Forrester.

Tory walked over to him and said, "I'm sure she will be fine. Don't forget she was at the base of the pier and probably got away at the first signs of the attack. But thank you for saving our lives," she leaned in and kissed Chris as a tear fell from her eye and landed on his cheek.

Natalie Forrester also thanked Chris and then the door burst open.

"Any first aid supplies or medical equipment in here?" called out the paramedics as they came through the door.

"We need any and everything you got," said a second medic.

"Hey Paul, it's me, Chris," he said to the second paramedic.

"Oh thank God, Chris! Could you give us a hand, we gotta a helluva mess out there?" Paul pleaded.

"Go ahead and go, we'll be fine," said Tory. Dr. Forrester and Natalie just nodded.

"All right, I'll call you later. I think I am going to need a good stiff drink at dinner," Chris said to Dr. Forrester as he gathered up supplies.

"I'm buying tonight," said Dr. Forrester, "We'll see you later."

Chris and the other two paramedics ran back toward the pier. As they arrived, Chris saw the carnage he only imagined moments before. Chris saw Angie briefly being administered to and at least knew she was alive and seemed better than most. When he got to the pier, it was

difficult to walk from slipping on all the spilled blood.
Every plank was saturated with it.

One of the TV cameras was panning the scene and
started recording the pandemonium right after the
attack. "This will never hit the airways, as it is too
graphic for the public news, but perhaps law
enforcement can use this to review what happened,"
said the announcer.

"Did you get any of the attacks?" asked a deputy.

"Not much, we were cowering and ducking in the
van," he said, "We knew we wouldn't last five minutes
out there, I'm extremely sorry."

"No need," said the deputy, "We have quite enough
victims already."

Corpses had already been loaded into body bags and
were being staged for later transport on the sand by the
road. The medics escorted some of the less seriously
injured to the restaurant where Chris had first sat and
talked with Lt. Ferguson.

Chris was attending to a young man with multiple
gashes. He suddenly felt a hand on his shoulder, and as
he turned around, he saw the tall figure that was Lt.
Ferguson smiling down on him.

"Thank God you're okay. Are Tory and Dr. Forrester
all right as well?" asked Lt. Ferguson.

"Yeah, we made it to the guard office," he said,
"Unlike so many others. I can't believe this, Lt.
Ferguson. There were thousands. They just fell like a
huge boulder on us."

Lt. Ferguson nodded and said, "Yes I know. Listen,

the CDC will be here shortly. Dr. Alice Friedman called me, and she is assembling a team. Once they get here, I'd like to talk to you about this if you can?"

"Just let me attend to some of the injured here until they come and I'll be all yours," he answered.

Lt. Ferguson nodded and said "I'll be at the restaurant. That's our command post."

Chris finished patching up the deeper cuts on the man before him and said he should walk over to the restaurant for more aid.

The next person he moved to was missing an eye and had a couple of deep slits on the side of her nose. She was a woman in her late thirties and could only cry as Chris spoke to her.

"My husband, he fell over the rail. I think he's dead. My husband is dead," she kept saying this and Chris realized that in addition to her wounds, she suffered from shock. He called for a blanket or some form of covering. After stemming her bleeding, Chris asked her to lie down even though there was nothing but blood around them. One of the other paramedics brought a blanket and something to elevate the legs.

Soon another army pulled up to the beach. There was an army of nurses, doctors and medical assistants that began running to the first unattended injuries they saw. Chris had assisted with five injuries and held the hand of one man who succumbed to his injuries and died from his massive blood loss.

By now Chris had as much blood on him as many of the casualties. He looked pale and was in denial as to what he witnessed. Chris had no military experience but thought that this qualified as such. Surely this was as bad as any battle the lifeguard read about from before. A shudder came to him as he thought, And this is not over! Where and when will the next attack happen?

He walked into the restaurant and moved passed the makeshift triage to the back knowing that is where Lt. Ferguson would set up shop. Sure enough, he sat at a table in the corner. Tory was seated across from him. She turned and took one look at Chris and gasped.

Chris quickly held up his clean previously gloved hand and said, "Don't worry, it's not from me. Sorry I couldn't stop to get cleaned up."

Lt. Ferguson said, "No problem with me. Sadly, I am starting to get used to it. Tory filled me in already about what happened for the most part. I didn't get to ask her before, so I'll ask you both. Did you happen to see what direction the birds came from?"

Chris answered first, "They were circling when we saw them, and I didn't see any birds join them after we noticed them."

"And the gulls were floating on the water, we never noticed them fly in," added Tory.

"The birds at the base of the pier just flew straight up off the roofs and trees. I don't think we even saw them before that, as we were almost to the end of the pier," finished Chris.

Lt. Ferguson scribbled something and then said, "As bad as all this is, I am concerned about where they went and when they may return."

"I thought about that, too. And I admit it has me scared," said Chris.

"Well if there is any good news in this, it seems that the attacks are taking place a couple of days after a previous ambush. That at least may give us a little time to work out something," said Tory.

"Like what?" asked Lt. Ferguson.

She shrugged and said, "I honestly don't know."

"I didn't see any birds outside," the lieutenant began to say.

"That's because they gorged themselves and flew off," said Tory with disgust, "Even the sparrows were in the assault."

Lt. Ferguson patted Tory's hand and said, "Try not to think about this too hard. I am sorry I wasn't here to assist. I wish I had been here to finally take those shots that you held me back from the other day. Perhaps I could have prevented a couple of those gulls from attacking today. And now I wonder which of us was really in the right?"

Tory said in response to his question, "We were, naturally."

For the first time today Lt. Ferguson chuckled. He asked, "I don't suppose you witnessed the direction they flew off to when they left?"

"From what little I saw, only that they headed inland," said Tory, "They seemed to be flying in three directions and not heading anywhere together."

Tory's phone rang, and she saw it was Prof. Revere. She answered it.

"I saw it on the news, or at least what they dared to show, are you all right?" said Prof. Revere in a high pitch Tory hadn't heard before.

"Yes, we're okay, just a little rattled. Dr. Forrester's wife got cut by a bird, and he took her straight away to the hospital to see Dr. Abernathy, but the three of us escaped without a mark thanks to Chris' quick wit."

"I like that young man even more than before if that's possible. Can we meet somewhere and talk about this? It may seem a little perverse, but I need to hear all the gory details. We have to figure out a way to stop this, and immediately," Prof. Revere said in a rapid speech.

"Lt. Ferguson was saying the same thing," said Tory, "It honestly looks like a battlefield here, and there are so many more dead and injured than I would have thought possible."

"The news station said they were setting up a triage station at Camp Pendleton and moving all the injured and sorting the deceased for identification. They said the hospitals were overflowing with patients and were asking everyone to avoid going there at all costs, until at least tomorrow," reported Prof. Revere.

"Especially since everyone who received even a scratch like Natalie will need treatment for rabies. And from what I heard from Dr. Forrester a little while ago, Dr. Abernathy told him they still do not have an optimal vaccine to cure, or even stop, the disease," Tory said.

They picked a place to meet up in a couple of hours,

as to allow Chris to get cleaned up and both of them take a shower. Prof. Revere said she would call Dr. Forrester and check on Natalie and see if they could meet up as well.

Lt. Ferguson had finished his questions and said they could head out and suggested they get some rest. "You both have had a traumatic day."

They drove back to Chris' house. The whole time they headed there, Tory thought of how close to death they had just come. She reflected on how many accomplishments and events that she would miss in her life had she died. But mostly, Tory thought about her chances to be loved by the man sitting next to her, and how she almost lost him as well. A tear ran down her face at both the terror she just witnessed and the thought of what she nearly lost. She swept it away before Chris could see it.

As they entered the kitchen, Chris spied a note hanging on the refrigerator. Steve wrote that he got called in to help assist victims of the bird attack. He would be at Camp Pendleton if Chris needed him for any reason. Chris had already reported in earlier, so Steve knew his roommate was safe.

"Seems we have the place to ourselves," Chris said and relayed the scribbled note to Tory. "I got to get out of these blood-soaked clothes."

They walked into his bedroom, which contained an

attached bath. She said as they went, "You know you probably ruined these clothes. I don't think the stains will ever come out."

"Oh well, it's about time I got some new clothes anyway, but I agree," he was thinking about how many people he was carrying on these clothes, some dead and some near to death.

"Yuck, let me help you with that," Tory said and came over to help him.

"Better still, please get me a trash bag from under the sink. These are going out immediately," Chris said, anxious to remove any evidence of the day's events.

"There is so much blood, what did you do, roll in it?" she asked as she retrieved the bag from the kitchen.

As she returned and gave the bag to Chris, he said, "Well I didn't have a lot of choices as everyone was laying on the pier. I had to get under their bodies..." He just trailed off thinking of all the victims.

"Never mind. Try not to dwell on it," she said feeling guilty that because of her questions he was reliving the horror. He got down to his briefs and turned the shower on, almost as hot as he could stand it.

Tory went into the living room and turned on the television. Every channel was talking about the attack. Most carried warnings of graphic images. As she watched the reports, she got a taste of what Chris had been dealing with the carnage the news showed. One channel even showed Chris momentarily treating one of the victims.

She thought again about all the death and

destruction the birds had wreaked. She was thinking about how they could stop them when she heard the water shut off. She decided to go back to his bedroom and warned Chris she was coming in.

He was still in the bathroom, and there was a good deal of steam coming from it. Tory said, "You made the news, or at least your blood-soaked back did."

He just grunted at the comment and then said, "Have you come up with any ideas on how to stop this? I can't think of any way to prevent the next attack, let alone where it may take place."

Tory laid on the bed and put her arm over her head, "I have been wondering about that myself, and I haven't come up with anything. I remember them flying off in three points of the compass. And that didn't make sense to me either as you would have thought they would stay together."

Chris came out of the shower feeling better, even if not great. He was clad only in a clean pair of briefs. "You know with all the terror we've been through today; I feel a little guilty. But I also can't help feeling relieved that we are alive and safe." He moved to the bed and laid down next to Tory.

"Mostly due to your quick thinking, but yes, I have been thinking of that as well," said Tory.

"If anything had happened to you..." he started to say, but she put two fingers to his lips and said, "Don't say it. This danger isn't over yet, and I don't want to put any words in the air."

When she took her fingers away, he leaned over and

kissed her fully. They kissed passionately, whether out of desire or thankfulness to be alive didn't matter. After such a near-death experience they decided not to allow their passion to wait another moment.

Tory unbuttoned her blouse, and Chris helped her out of it. She unfastened her bra and removed it. She slid his briefs off him and began caressing his body. He lowered her panties, and then they laid there holding each other for a little while as if taking stock of everything. After a few more moments they began to make love.

A little over an hour later they hadn't gotten any rest, but they both felt exhilarated and satiated. At one point Tory began crying for all those who had lost their lives or loved ones. Chris comforted her and said this was a time to be thankful for each other, and the fact that they would still face tomorrow together. After a couple of deep breaths and some gentle caresses by Chris, she felt better.

They were supposed to meet Prof. Revere in about a half hour, so Tory moved slowly off the bed and away from Chris. She started to get dressed, and Chris just watched her smiling.

"You are quite beautiful, you know," he said to her.

"You're not too hard on the eyes either," she teased him, feeling a little more like her old self.

He laughed and then turned serious and said, "You know, perhaps you could save the college some money and stay here instead. Steve wouldn't mind, as I already asked him."

"We can talk about that later, but I promise I'll give that some careful thought," she said, knowing she already had been doing that, "But for now we have to get going. So are you getting out of that bed or do I have to come drag you out of it?"

"Okay, I'll get moving, but you know I would rather stay here this afternoon with you," he said hopefully.

"I'll come back with you this evening," she said, "But we promised Prof. Revere we'd meet up with her."

"I have to say I am getting sick and tired of dealing with these rabid birds all the time," said Chris, "I hope and pray we come up with a solution soon. Especially before anyone else loses their life."

"That makes two of us. Not to mention I'd like to get back to some nice quiet research again," Tory said in a frustrated voice.

"Are you going to continue your studies in this field after all this?" he asked her.

"Yes, even though there may be thousands of them, I'm not letting this group of bad apples spoil my whole career. Besides, I can't blame the birds for getting sick. They are only doing what their current nature tells them," she said.

Chris thought that Mother Nature needed a severe talking to after what they just escaped. He saw that Tory was setting her jaw, and since they had shared such a beautiful, intimate time, he didn't want to destroy the mood. He pulled some clean clothes out of his dresser and said, "Let's go see Prof. Revere and see if we can't find a way to reform these wayward creatures."

Prof. Revere had called as they began to pull away from Chris' house. All five of them, including Natalie Forrester, agreed to meet at the hotel the Forresters were staying. They pulled into the parking lot 20 minutes later.

As they entered, there was a significant breakfast area that was currently uninhabited except for Dr. and Mrs. Forrester. Fresh coffee was always ready, and Dr. Forrester was holding a cup with both hands looking down into the steaming liquid when Chris and Tory came in.

"How are you feeling?" Tory asked Natalie before saying anything else.

"Sore. The vaccination was far more painful than the injury if you can even qualify it like that," she said attempting a smile.

Prof. Revere came in from the other side just as Natalie Forrester was talking and when she finished Prof. Revere said, "Well thank heavens you all are all right! I'd heard that there were dozens of casualties and dozens more injured."

"They are playing it down," said Chris quietly, "I know, I saw. There had to be at least a couple hundred dead that I saw, and they had already begun piling up the body bags before I got there."

"My God!" exclaimed Prof. Revere.

"I don't think anyone had ever seen anything like it," said Dr. Forrester, "The whole pier went dark when they came out of the sky. There must have been 5,000 birds if there was one."

"That's incredible," Prof. Revere was aghast at the thought, "And all of them attacked?"

"To the very last feather," answered Chris, "And they knew to ambush the pier where no one could get away from them."

"Which begs the question, how the hell could they know there would be all those people today?" asked Dr. Forrester, "They KNEW, the birds utterly knew – and they also planned. They set up their ranks on three fronts, east, west and directly above."

Prof. Revere looked at Dr. Forrester and said softly, "Maybe it just seemed that way. Perhaps they were gathering in that area like at the train station."

"I'm sorry Prof. Revere," said Chris, "They knew what they were doing. And they waited, biding their time and gathering strength. When the pier was practically at a standstill because there were so many people, that's when they hit us. There was distinct strategies and a tactic to all this. And they knew it, just like Dr. Forrester said."

Prof. Revere looked at Tory, and she just looked back at her and nodded her head, "It's true."

"Then this is as bad as I thought it might get," said Prof. Revere, "And the chances of stemming or even slowing it are getting smaller each day."

"We haven't even seen any recent nesting activity around this area. The hope of finding that cockatoo is nothing short of impossible," said Dr. Forrester, "My students were at it all day yesterday. Thankfully they all left before this morning."

Natalie told them, "I'm concerned about what Doctor Abernathy said. He hoped that the vaccine he gave me would prevent the disease from taking hold, but he didn't sound very optimistic. He said that frankly without a stronger vaccine for this antigen, it may not be cured."

"Without the host or finding another species that has resilient antibodies against the strain, they can't develop a stronger antidote than what they already have," said Dr. Forrester.

"What else?" asked Tory, she could feel they were holding back, She wanted to know what more they were unwilling to say.

"Dr. Abernathy said that if they could not find the host, the only other possibility was to find an animal that had a natural immunity to the disease. They need to develop T-cells from it that could combat the disease since ours can't" explained Dr. Forrester.

For a moment everyone was quiet.

Suddenly Tory's eyes went wide, and she yelled out, "Pelicans!"

Everyone at the table jumped, and Dr. Forrester said, "Tory, you are going to have to learn some restraint before just blurting something out loud like that."

Prof. Revere chuckled at this, and Tory apologized, but then said, "You said every bird seems to be affected by this rabies strain, all but pelicans!"

"She's right," said Prof. Revere, "There has not been a single pelican that seems to be infected, and none included in any of the attacks we have seen."

"And the gulls attacked the pelican, not the other way around, which we are guessing wouldn't be usual if they were susceptible or carrying the rabies disease," said Tory excited at this new possibility.

"Perhaps they just haven't been exposed to the disease in the same way as other species," reasoned Dr. Forrester.

"Possibly, but we should take some blood from one of the infected specimens and inject a pelican to see if they have a natural immunity to the virus," said Prof. Revere now catching Tory's enthusiasm, "They may have the natural antibodies that might reject and even destroy the virus."

Dr. Forrester thought for a moment and looked at his wife. He smiled and said, "Let's get us some pelicans."

"I am going to call Lt. Ferguson and let him know we might have an alternative to hunting down the cockatoo," said Tory.

"I wouldn't put too many eggs in this basket yet," Dr. Forrester said to her, "It is just a theory right now, and we may wind up with a couple of very sick pelicans and nothing more."

"Yes, perhaps we shouldn't notify the Sheriff's office with our theory until it is more than that," said Prof. Revere, "While I must admit that it might seem hopeless, we might still catch a break and find the remains of the cockatoo. Even a little bone marrow from that bird could develop a vaccine if it turns out that the pelicans aren't immune to the pathogen."

Tory set her phone back down and said, "Yeah, I

guess I am getting a little ahead of myself."

"Well I for one don't blame you, and I hope you are right. I know there are a couple of pelican rescue sanctuaries in this region and I will call them," said Dr. Forrester. He was more upbeat than he was a few moments ago.

"I believe the zoological society has a few of them as well. I'll reach out to the vet's staff and find out," added Tory.

"Who knows," said Prof. Revere in a hopeful voice, "We may be looking at the McKnight SARV Vaccine."

CHAPTER 15 – DAY 21

There was no longer any possibility of keeping the bird attacks under wraps. All of the local and most of the national TV stations had shared an edited version of the videotape. There was a full alert to beware of aggressive birds hovering around the south coast.

The count as of Sunday morning was 183 dead and nearly 1,000 injured. The extent of the injuries ranged from minor cuts like Natalie's to the critically injured with little hope for survival. The CDC anticipated a death toll exceeding 300 before the next 48 hours elapsed.

Dr. Friedman had done a press release advising that if anyone received any wounds or injuries from any bird to please seek immediate medical attention at the nearest urgent care or their doctor's offices. She knew it was long past too late to keep this under wraps, and that the time had come to make sure they saw everyone who might be infected.

Another plane full of CDC personnel would be arriving from Atlanta to assist, and the word had been put out to the medical community in three states, Arizona, Nevada and all of California, to be on the lookout for any signs of rabies and to alert the CDC at a disclosed emergency number.

They were now worried that the birds might spread

from the South Coast area into other parts of Southern California and beyond. Especially considering the number of birds involved in the attack on Saturday.

The governor declared a state of emergency for Orange County, and there were now several armored vehicles from Camp Pendleton searching for any concentration of birds flocking together. Most notably if they contained more than one species in the group.

Because of the media, there were now many trigger-happy residents that shot up several power lines and knocked out electricity, phone, and internet in a few neighborhoods. They were firing at birds sitting on those lines. The couple birds they hit were later shown to be free of disease. The complaints from residents and the power and phone companies were constant.

People were urged to let the military and deputies handle the problem, and contact them instead of taking matters into their own hands.

Meanwhile, the soldiers had checked the industrial park after a flood of phone calls had placed the birds there on Friday. There were no birds found in the area, including what would typically be there on any given day.

Once again, the birds had disappeared.

Monday saw a cancellation of the area schools. The public was warned to avoid areas where birds of any substantial number might be congregating. A hotline was established to report flocks of birds higher than ten or more individuals together. Residents were asked to discontinue feeding birds for the time being and discouraged to have contact with them.

In Orange County, terror gripped residents at the reports coming in along with further updates of the attack. Interviews and replays of the train incident flooded the news. Reports had now tied the two assaults together.

The only part that was held in check was the rabies problem, although rumors began floating around that the birds obviously had something seriously wrong with them. The newspeople stated that only a grave disease would cut across so many species and cause so much wanton aggression.

The press was not allowed to interview patients and witnesses in the hospitals or urgent care systems for the sake of their privacy. There were guards posted at every facility to ensure this. But enough patients ran around that it did not take long for the words the words "aviary rabies" to be bantered through the halls.

In addition to the military, Homeland Security had been brought in to make sure a panic and a subsequent riot did not break out in the communities. The entire county was under close watch by the government, and it was keeping any information as closely guarded as they could.

Dr. Forrester contacted the pelican rescue organization and explained to them that it was a matter of human lives at stake. They suspected that it might have something to do with the attack of yesterday, but Dr. Forrester would say nothing further. They only had the one female.

Tory was able to secure both a female and male from the zoological society after numerous phone calls on a Sunday.

Dr. Forrester's students would be able to pick up the three birds on Monday and would take them to a lab that was being set up at SDSU. Prof. Revere would accompany Dr. Forrester, while Chris and Tory would attempt to learn where the birds had disappeared.

Dr. Friedman was alerted to the hope that pelicans might be resilient to the rabies virus, and that they would be checking on this new possibility. Dr. Friedman also assigned an epidemiologist, veterinarian, and microbiologist to assist them in the lab. They, and anyone else were at Dr. Forrester and Prof. Revere's disposal.

As they headed south to the campus, Dr. Forrester asked Prof. Revere, "Even if we find a new vaccine how could we possibly administer it to thousands of birds that fly off to who knows where?"

"First things first," she answered, "Let's see if we can't save Natalie, and those lying in the hospital, and then we can figure out how to inoculate the birds."

"Do you agree with Tory's assessment that we have today and tomorrow until we see another ambush?" he asked her.

"She may be right, and I hope for everyone's sake we have at least these two days," she answered, "But in any event, I don't think we'll have enough time, especially after the severity of the last attack. If you think 5,000 birds were involved, how many might there be in another week?"

"They aren't dying off as we had hoped they would, and did, in Bodega Bay, are they?" he asked.

"Apparently not in any large numbers," she said, "As I feared, I believe we are looking at a much more virulent strain than from before. I think some of the weaker birds are succumbing to the disease, but if it was a healthy bird, to begin with, maybe it can resist the fatality of the disease for quite a time longer."

"Why can't we humans fend it off, then? We seem to be dropping much faster than the birds are. That doesn't make sense to me," he complained.

"Perhaps it's because, between the birds and us, a bird's metabolism is higher. I don't know," Prof. Revere said at a loss, "Maybe it's because we were already susceptible to rabies in the first place."

"Please God let us save Natalie in time," he said, rubbing his eyes.

"We will. Have some faith, Bill; I think we may be closer to finding that cure now. And at least she got immediate treatment," she said with as much confidence as she could muster.

Deciding to change the subject, Prof. Revere thought this as good a time as any. "Bill, I want to talk to you about something else since we have the time..."

Chris and Tory were driving around in Tory's jeep. While they had been a little worried about it, they decided to take the top off the vehicle so they could see better in all directions.

"Okay, but I hope you can pull a Mario Andretti if the need arises," said Chris before they left.

Ordinarily, Chris would have relished the open vehicle. But things weren't ordinary anymore. He brought along his binoculars, as he hoped he would see the gathering birds long before they were on them. He also hoped that Tory's hypothesis was correct about being a couple of days in between attacks.

They had looked again in some of the spots where they had assembled previously and had not spied them anywhere. They drove to the mall. Only a few sparrows were flying around, which did not seem suspicious. After spending most of the day chasing down possible targets of concentration they decided to call it a day and head out again tomorrow.

On the complete opposite side of San Clemente somewhere in the middle of the marine base lay an abandoned building used for practice maneuvers and exercises. It was four stories tall, and every floor was filled with birds.

The hawks and falcons were on the roof looking for any signs of disturbances. A couple of rabbits had ventured out in the brush, but they were left unmolested by the birds since they were still bloated from the feast the day before. Although they always felt the urge to cram more down their gullet, they were so full that they didn't feel much like flying.

Anyone would have been astounded by the vast

number and types of birds. With their attack and enormous appetite satiated, they walked around the building dropping excrement everywhere. Any birds in the area visiting the building after they left were bound to get a healthy new dose of rabies.

Some of the infected birds, though no less full than the others, were still scouting around the area. They came upon the main base and all its shops downtown. They saw many people bustling about trying to run errands and take care of their business.

It was a typical day at the base. But something was catching their attention, and that was the scent of mercaptan that the vultures picked up from the bodies not yet identified or claimed from Saturday. There was still food down there, just waiting to be picked over.

They did not fly in large groups but were more like scouts noting the comings and goings of the base. Each person paid no attention to the birds since there were only a few of them about, and everyone was warned to beware of large groups. That plus so far nothing had happened this far south.

Besides, where else could they be safer than at a military base?

Chapter 16 – Day 22

The students picked up and brought the pelicans to the lab. They had quite a fight on their hands as the rescue facility did not want to release the bird until they got better answers of what would happen to it. It wasn't until the rescue got a call from Homeland Security, when they finally, but grudgingly released their captive.

The zoological society was a more straightforward pickup, and by 11 that morning the three immediately available pelicans were in the lab at UCSD. The rabies strains were prepared earlier from several of the infected birds.

It wasn't easy for Prof. Revere or Dr. Forrester to infect the birds, but they knew it had to be done. As they injected the three birds with strains from three different hosts, they prayed silently that the birds would be able to reject the virus, and that up until then it hadn't been purely a matter of luck that they hadn't gotten the disease.

They wondered how long it would take to show signs of the infection. They were unsure how long this rabies virus took to infect and change the animal. They did suspect that it would take effect sooner than mammalian rabies, again due to the faster metabolism and higher temperatures, but they couldn't guess if that were a day or days.

They knew they were fighting against time. The birds might attack again as soon as tomorrow, with no clue as to where. And that was only if the "every third-day" theory of Tory's was accurate. The only good news was that there were no significant gatherings of people scheduled during the week. Schools remained closed until further notice, and any scheduled outings were either postponed or canceled for safety's sake.

This morning Tory and Chris were once more trying to find their elusive quarry. Tory had spent nearly every moment with Chris since the attack. Their time together wasn't making her decision any more comfortable.

Tory liked Chris' easy going and friendly attitude, but he didn't have the drive and ambition she did. He wasn't sure what he wanted to do with his life. Tory didn't have any final plans, although she had a pretty good idea what appealed to her, and that she was always anxious to go after things.

Many times in conversation, she tried to pin Chris down to some possible career choice for him going forward, but he was like a tumbleweed in a Texas twister. He was enjoying what he was doing now, and that was good enough for him for the time being.

Chris was a passionate lover and interesting to talk to, but she knew that wouldn't last into their later years. Once more, Tory decided to go along with the situation for the moment. She figured the answer would present itself in time.

They cleared a hill on the other side of the industrial center where the birds had concentrated last Friday. As they were following the trail, it came to a barbed wire fence that held a big sign across the road barring entrance.

It stated that the property belonged to Camp Pendleton and only authorized personnel were allowed. It also contained a second sign declaring the area as a live fire test area.

"Well, I guess that's posted clear enough," said Chris.

"Chris, do you have your binoculars?" said Tory squinting off into the distance.

"Yeah, what do you see?" he asked.

"There is a building way off there, and I think it is moving," she answered.

"What do you mean? Buildings don't move," he thought she was teasing him.

"I think this one is, and I think we found our feathered friends," she replied.

As she brought the binoculars to her eyes and adjusted them, she found herself staring at several hawks that were staring back. She looked at the rest of the building and returned to the hawks. She saw the first one unfurl its wings and take off.

"Oh shit," she said and as fast as her reflexes allowed she put the Jeep in reverse and headed back the way she came.

"What happened?" asked Chris. Before he could take a look, the vehicle was moving backward and then spun around, and Tory was making tracks for the town as fast as the Jeep could pick up speed.

"I think we were spotted and they have decided to

investigate," was all she said.

Chris turned around in his seat and tried to spot anything coming toward them, "Tory, I don't see anything. Oh wait, yes I do. I see three of them," he said, "And yeah, they are heading in our direction."

"Hang on, one Mario Andretti coming up," she said although quite seriously. She floored the Jeep and was almost back to the industrial center.

"You can't go this fast through the commercial center, we will plow into something or someone," he pleaded.

"I saw a building with an underground loading dock, I am heading for that just to get out of sight from those hawks."

She took the corner on two wheels on her side as the Jeep momentarily left the road. The car grabbed it again a second later. Chris' knuckles were white as he held tightly to the assist handle. She banked left and pulled into the large pharmacy manufacturer's parking lot. She went to the back of the structure and saw at what she was aiming.

She slowed and pulled alongside the loading dock parking parallel to the dock. She killed the engine and told Chris to get out. He didn't hesitate, and the two of them ran up to the door at the dock and knocked softly.

A couple of moments later the door opened, and a smallish man in a white lab coat said, "Receiving is closed."

"Good," answered Tory and pushed the door and the man aside.

"Hey!" the man exclaimed.

"We have birds after us," Chris explained rapidly, "We need to get inside and away from them, as we are out in the open in that car."

"How many?" asked the man still upset with their forced entry.

"Several large red-tailed hawks," answered Tory.

"Just a few hawks? I heard these things attacked by the thousands," the man snickered.

"Well, Mr. … Church," Tory said reading his badge, "Why don't you step outside and let them know you don't consider them any threat? And after you chase them off, we will be on our way."

"Mr. Church," said Chris in a calm voice, "I work for the county, and I could see we were in trouble, now we are just asking for a little sanctuary until those birds return to wherever they were before they decided to chase us."

"What do you do for the county?" asked Church suspiciously.

"I am a lifeguard and paramedic," he answered.

"Well this is a secure facility, and trespassers are not allowed to walk our halls unescorted," Church puffed up his chest trying to look as official as he sounded.

"Fine," said Tory, "You may escort us to the lobby, and we will wait until the birds have left and then we will return to our vehicle."

Church thought for a moment and then said, "Well if you believe you are in danger, I suppose I can do that."

"We would appreciate it," said Chris.

"All right, follow me," and with that Church took them through several halls to a door that led to the large atrium.

He spoke to the receptionist and explained the situation. She nodded and said to the couple, "Please make yourself at home and stay as long as you wish until you feel safe."

"You are very kind," said Tory and then she thanked Church for his help. He nodded, turned and left.

"Don't mention it," said the receptionist, "My best friend was seriously injured last Saturday from that attack. She's still in the hospital, it's awful."

They both just nodded and Tory said, "I'm sorry."

Chris looked out the tall lobby windows into the sky and saw nothing but a couple of small clouds rolling by. He watched for several minutes, and the scene didn't change.

"Perhaps I should take a look outside?" he said.

"Be careful, these things seem more intelligent then even I give them credit for being. Almost like the disease made them smarter," Tory whispered to him, "In the meantime, I am going to call Lt. Ferguson and let him know that we found a large gathering of birds."

"Yeah, tell him this time he can truly send in the Marines as they're in their backyard!" chuckled Chris more out of nervousness than humor.

He moved to the door and walked out into the adjacent parking lot. He almost ran into a small tree as he was looking at the roof and sky for any traces of winged creatures. He adjusted at the last moment and barely missed it. He couldn't see anything posing a threat. There wasn't a single bird of any kind around the area.

He was beginning to think Tory might have mistaken about them coming after them. Then he saw a hawk circling way up in the sky. It was flying solo, but Chris knew it was searching for something. Whether it was them or not he wasn't sure, but he wouldn't want to chance it.

He thought if they waited about fifteen minutes it might go off to another area. He returned to the lobby. As Chris entered, he could see Tory was on the phone.

"Tell them they are looking for a deserted building close to the industrial park," she said into the device, "All types, and they looked to be all over it. No, we won't head back there." She was looking at Chris now, and he shook his head. "Chris didn't see anything, perhaps they returned to the roost, so we're okay."

After a few more seconds and words, she hung up. "Lt. Ferguson said he would contact the base commander and notify him of what we saw. He is sure that they can get a squad of men out there in short order."

"There was only one hawk circling way up there like they normally do," said Chris, "The others probably headed back."

"You do know hawks can see more than a mile away as clearly as I am looking at you now?" she asked him.

"I guess I do now," he said, "but he didn't move toward me, he just kept circling."

"He doesn't have to; he can see you and every move you make," she answered him, "I wish I had his eyesight to know if any of the birds had moved from that building."

A couple of moments later Tory's phone sprang to life, and she saw Lt. Ferguson was calling. "Hi, what's up?" she listened carefully and responded, "I've got it, about 15 minutes, we'll head out. Thanks." She hung up the phone.

"Well?" asked Chris.

"Seems the Marines are coming to the rescue. They are going to fire missiles into that abandoned building and then send a full battalion to wipe out the rest of the birds," she said matter-of-factly.

"Look, Tory, I know that's not how you want it, but really what alternative do we have? Especially if they choose to attack again tomorrow, or possibly later today?" he asked.

She just nodded her head and said, "I told Lt. Ferguson we would leave the area, but I am wondering, maybe we should see what happens...to make sure I mean?" she asked Chris.

"Oh no you don't," he immediately answered her, "You aren't going to catch shrapnel, or a piece of flying debris, just to satisfy your curiosity. Besides if any birds do escape, we won't know what's on their diseased minds. I think this time we check the news at 11, instead."

She saw his grave concern and said, "Let's compromise. We'll go up to the top of that hill." She pointed through the windows to an incline that was the apex of the industrial park. "If we can see the building with your high powered binoculars, we'll stay there. If not, we will have to get closer so we can see what happens."

Chris thought he might at least have a chance this way, as he knew Tory wouldn't give up otherwise. At least he could protect her from a ringside seat this way. He nodded his head and quietly said, "Agreed."

They decided to chance the hawk that was circling and went around the building to Tory's car. She drove up to the top of the hill undisturbed. They could make out the building and see the birds moving around it with Chris' binoculars. They were both satisfied with the compromise.

Lt. Colonel Jack Carretti had put out the order. He had three companies consisting of three to five platoons each. A total of 475 marines total. This group was his mop-up battalion to make sure that if any birds were still living after the missile attack, they wouldn't be for long.

Lt. Col. Carretti was 5-foot-9-inches, a solid 180 pounds and had just turned 43. His face chiseled, and his hair as closely shaved as his face. He was every ounce a marine and logged 23 plus years in the corps.

He was ordered to make certain that any of these rabid birds came to a complete end before they could commence another onslaught similar to last Saturday's carnage. He had seen that devastation first hand, and was ready for some payback. He knew people were still dying from their injuries from that debacle, and that many more infected by their dangerous disease.

The officer lived in San Clemente with his wife, Katherine, for nearly 22 years. Thankfully she had friends that came last weekend and stayed with them. Katherine talked about going to the festival until they called. She even entertained the thought of taking her friends to the event. She decided since she hadn't seen them in such a long time she preferred to put a big brunch on for them instead.

Lt. Col. Carretti thought many times since then how close Katherine and her friends came to be a number from that fateful day. He also thought how many others didn't change their plans and now, if they were alive at all, the hell they were going through to stay alive.

The marines readied their surface-to-surface missiles. They knew the coordinates for the exercise area that held the building from previous exercises. Carretti visited that building numerous times on practice maneuvers. They were using three FGM-148 Javelins, a fire-and-forget missile with lock-on before launch, and automatic self-guidance. The system takes a top-attack flight profile against armored vehicles (attacking the top armor, which is thinner), but also uses a direct-attack mode for use against stable structures such as this.

When his men were fully assembled and in their transports, he gave the order to fire the missiles. From another area of the camp, he heard the launch of the three Javelins. He looked over at the three projectiles and watched as their second propulsion systems kicked in and took the rockets streaking to their target.

The hawk that was circling above also witnessed the launch and screeched to the birds below. Just as a massive billowing of wings began, the first rocket struck the building's third floor. Steel and concrete flew in every direction. Then the second and third missiles hit the rest of the building one on the first floor and the last on the roof. Each warhead consisted of a shape charge which is designed to cut through heavy armor and cause the most damage.

The building obliterated instantly. Few birds escaped before the missiles struck, the majority was taken out from an explosion of the steel and concrete. Shrapnel and debris flew everywhere and killed the birds before they could make good their escape.

Lt. Col. Carretti mobilized his men upon the first impact. He did not want to take the chance that any infected birds would get away to contaminate other birds or people later on. He was less than a kilometer from the area and knew he could cover that distance in under 2 minutes, on the makeshift road leading to the building.

A cloud of dust was both in front and behind the units. The soldiers were already locked and loaded and told to watch for any birds that might have gotten away or blown clear of the initial blast. The Sgt.-Major had told the men that anything that even looked like a bird should be "disposed of" with extreme prejudice, as it had to be infected if it was anywhere near them.

Carretti had the binoculars to his eyes, but he only saw a cloud of dust where the building once stood. They were almost on top of the building, and he still could not see what was left, or if anything was moving through the cloud of dust. He ordered the vehicles to slow. Nothing was flying above the structure except one hawk that was apparently too high and out of range to shoot.

As they pulled up and began unloading, Carretti could see numerous dead birds laying on the ground. He started to hear the popping of gunfire around the location and saw a few flashes as the soldiers made sure the birds were dead.

"All right, spread the men out sargent.-major and have them comb the area in earnest for any survivors," he shouted to his sargent.

"You heard the man! If we find so much as a twitching claw, the soldier that missed it will be eating that bird for dinner. Do you understand me?"

"Yes, sargent-major!" The company responded as one.

Carretti was bothered that because of the speed of the attack, he never saw how many birds there might have been before the missile strike. So now he didn't know how many remained and how many there was in the beginning. He understood the urgency to hit the target before it changed, but it didn't make not knowing how many survived any easier.

He looked up at the hawk, but if it knew anything more than he did, it wasn't letting on. It hadn't changed direction or moved away from its circle. It just hovered over his men and what remained of the building. It's as if it was trying to determine the damage itself. As Carretti assessed the damage, he heard a car horn sound and spun around. There were two people signaling to him from the other side of the protective fence and road that lead to the industrial center.

Carretti told the corporal in his jeep to run him over there. As he got to the fence, he began yelling at the couple saying that they are dangerously close to a military maneuver and that their heads could have been blown off.

"I am sorry, sir. I wanted to let you know what happened," Tory called back, "We saw the explosion and thought you might want some Intel on what you got and what you missed."

Chris was even more apologetic but added that it was them that called in the strike and that they were involved in the whole incident from the start. "Honest Colonel, we want to help you any way we can," Chris finished.

Carretti softened and said, "It's Lieutenant Colonel Jack Carretti," and after a pause, "All right tell me what you know."

Chris and Tory said they were up on the hill closest to the industrial center and could see the building with Chris' binoculars. They told Carretti that just before the explosions they watched numerous birds fly off.

"The explosions took a good many of them out, but quite a few flew the opposite way the rockets hit, and many got clear of the bombings.

"Any idea how many is 'many'?" asked Carretti to Chris.

"I saw two vultures, about 15 gulls, a few mockingbirds, and some smaller birds, perhaps 20-30 that I couldn't determine from the smoke and dust that followed," answered Tory.

"You're quite the bird watcher, aren't you, young lady?" said Lt. Col. Carretti to Tory.

"I am in the Ornithology program at SDSU, and I'm also working on a migratory program through San Diego Zoological Society in San Clemente," she said rapidly.

"My apologies for my brusqueness," Lt. Col. Carretti answered, "Could you track which direction they were heading?"

"Mostly North-northeast, they looked to be heading inland and back toward San Clemente," she said.

"Any idea why he's hanging around?" Lt. Col. Carretti pointed to the lone hawk circling the remains of the building.

"I think he is watching to see what you are going to do next," she guessed and shrugged, "Before you showed up he was chasing us."

"Really?" asked Lt. Col. Carretti, "Are you sure it was the same one?"

"One of three that flew off that building you bombed," answered Chris, "We got away in one of the buildings inside that industrial center."

"If he weren't so damn high up, I'd end his constant circling," Lt. Col. Carretti said.

"And I believe he knows that," said Tory.

Carretti scoffed and said, "Yeah, I'll bet he does."

"The good news is that you got the bulk of them, Lt. Colonel," said Chris, "But unfortunately not all of them. We still have infected birds on the wing."

Then the sizable red-tailed hawk quit circling and headed west toward the ocean.

"Where do you suppose he's headed?" asked Lt. Col. Carretti.

"He's just throwing you off the scent," answered Tory, "He probably expects one of your men to ask if they should follow it, which will take you further away from where the others went."

"You make them sound smarter than us," Lt. Col. Carretti scoffed again.

Chris rolled his eyes as Tory explained that in many ways, they were. Halfway through her explanation, a private ran up to the Colonel and advised him that the hawk, "flew off that away and that a bunch of the men thought we should follow him." Chris just smiled, and Lt. Col. Carretti looked at Tory who only shrugged again.

CHAPTER 17 - DAY 23

The bottom line of the retaliation by the Marines was that the missiles and troops took out more than 4,000 birds and less than 100 birds escaped the barrage. While it wasn't as simple and tidy as the Bodega Bay experience, it finally helped turn the tide against the birds.

By finally curbing the number of birds with the disease, everyone hoped that no sizable attacks similar to the Microbrew Festival would happen again. However single bird hostilities continued to take place. These happened all around the South Coast. People were now at least aware of the attacking birds and knew that if they were cut or scratched they needed to seek medical attention as quickly as possible.

With all the medical facilities filled, most new patients were being sent and treated at temporary medical offices. These makeshift triages were set up by the military and homeland security. There were now more than 675 people treated for rabies at nearly 35 addresses around Orange County.

The number of patients included more than 500 seriously injured people still in critical condition from the assaults at the church and the pier. The medical staff was still uncertain as to whether or not the wounded would survive their initial injuries, let alone the rabies infection beyond.

Dr. Forrester and Prof. Revere estimated that they were still a few days from knowing whether the pelicans were immune or not, but at least initially there seemed to be no immediate destruction of the cells from the rabies virus. It was the first time they had dared hope that a new and more powerful vaccine might develop from these birds.

Lt. Ferguson received a call from a resident that said she had seen more than 50 birds gathering at the Richard T. Steed Public Park, not too far from either the industrial park or Camp Pendleton. Lt. Ferguson quickly dialed up Under-Sheriff Puerta who called Lt. Colonel Carretti. Carretti completed the circle and phoned Ferguson to coordinate a military and deputies strike against the flocking birds.

Less than forty-five minutes later both types of vehicles sat just outside the entrance of the park. Lt. Ferguson told his deputies that they needed to sneak up on the birds this time and catch them before they flew off.

Lt. Col. Carretti had a better plan and brought up four soldiers each with a specialized mortar and ammunition. Carretti said, "These nets will cover a hundred-by-hundred foot area. We can trap them in the nets and then dispose of them safely after that."

"The lady said the birds were gathering on the concession stand in the middle of the park. What if they are also on the light stanchions or other fences? This park is riddled with those for the baseball fields,"

Lt. Ferguson asked the Lt. Colonel.

The officer thought for a moment and then turned to his sargent-major and said, "I need eyes in there. I need to know where those goddamned things are before we try to corral them."

Sargent-major Freeman said "Yessir," and moved to the back of the line.

While Carretti only had about half of the battalion he did for the last raid at the building, because the area was smaller and the birds fewer. But he had his best men and his trusted sargent-major with him. He watched as three of his soldiers began moving into the park. Carretti had trouble spotting them after going in a few feet from the entrance, their camouflage, and precise movements dissolved them into the trees.

About five minutes later the three soldiers reported back to Lt. Col. Carretti. The corporal did the talking, "Lt. Col. Carretti, you have nearly a hundred birds all perched on the concession stand roof. If we hit it from all four sides with the nets, we could catch them all, with almost none of them getting free or escaping. A couple of birds are seated on two of the high fences away from the concession stand on opposite sides. I figure a couple of snipers could take them out at the same time we fire the mortars. One is that damned hawk, and the other is a big crow."

Lt. Col. Carretti nodded and said to both Sgt. Freeman and his corporal, "Okay, get Gonzales and Peterson to take up a position to snipe each of the scout birds. Once they are in position, move the mortars in quietly. If we miss this, we may not get another chance."

"Understood, sir," answered Freeman in a whisper, then he nodded at the corporal and the two soldiers returned to the back of the line. Ferguson asked Carretti if there was anything he or his men could do to assist them.

"Yeah, stay close and make sure none of these damn things get away this time," he answered, "Hopefully we can bring an end to this thing today."

As the soldiers began to take up their positions, they watched the crow keel over from its perch on the line. As they looked over to the roof, the Marines noticed numerous birds were lying down on the roof and not moving.

"What the hell's going on?" one of the soldiers asked the other. The hawk began to fly off, but before one of the soldiers could aim his rifle at the bird, it stopped flapping its wings and fell to the ground. It lay dead on the grass by the field it perched near.

A few more birds fell off the roof and onto the concrete in front of the concession stand. The soldiers held their ground and just watched as if the birds were being picked off by a silent sniper before their eyes.

The Marines played it safe and shot their mortars capturing what remained of the birds. A few tried to fly off but got caught in the nets. Most of them stayed stationary and didn't have the will or strength to move. They shot any moving birds once the nets were secured and positive nothing could escape.

The die-off was not only happening at Steed Park but all over South Orange County. Birds were dropping from buildings, the sky, trees or just falling over on the ground. It was almost as if someone had flipped a switch and their bodies began crashing everywhere.

In truth, many of these birds became infected with the rabies disease nearly three weeks ago, and their nervous systems were breaking down and failing. If they had been mammals, this is when foaming at the mouth would be prevalent from involuntary increased saliva production. Since birds do not produce saliva, they just became disoriented and fell over, succumbing within minutes to the last vestiges of the disease, completely shutting down their nervous system.

There remained some birds with early stages of the disease, and these birds continued scavenging for anything they could find. But so many birds had died off from either being killed off or succumbed to the infection, that there were hardly any birds left in Orange County. Since the majority of these creatures spent all their time scavenging for food, they never left the general vicinity.

By staying put, it prevented the disease from migrating out of the area. The last birds that became infected were no less aggressive, but these were now fewer and smaller in size. Hardly seen was a bird of prey or seabird in the area. It was Bodega Bay all over again, but with a few differences.

The first of these was the body count. If no other persons lost their lives, which was unlikely, the number of the dead currently stood at 492. This count included those that died from the rabies infection earlier. Souls lost like Andy, Christy, and Rachel who were linked by the CDC office in Santa Ana. The death toll from the pier alone crossed north of 400 people, with many more clinging to life.

That was more than four times Bodega Bay.

The second difference was the number of species that were affected. Twenty-seven species had been identified compared to seven before.

The final difference was the severity of the rabies infection itself. While it could not be proven, it seemed inevitable that this pathogen was far more severe and poisonous than its predecessor.

Lt. Ferguson called Tory and reported what had taken place at Richard Steed Park. He said he had also heard from some of his other officers that other birds were falling all around the area. Tory made an audible sigh and said she prayed this event was finally over for everyone.

"Well everyone except the people infected with rabies," said Lt. Ferguson, "I spoke with Dr. Friedman yesterday afternoon, and she said that even with all of the rabies injections they have given out, people are not getting better. Have you heard anything from Dr. Forrester yet?"

"Nothing yet," she answered, "They injected the birds Monday, but said it might be a few days before we can see if anything happens with them. I'm sure they will call us either way as soon as they know something."

"Yeah," was all Lt. Ferguson could say to that, "Now listen, we aren't completely out of the woods yet, as there are still several birds swooping down on people, so don't let your guard down."

"Yes, Papa," said Tory teasingly, "I promise I'll be safe."

"Yeah and keep that boyfriend of yours protected as well." he finished and then said goodbye.

Tory thought that she might be able to help keep Chris physically safe. However, she was sure she would end up breaking his heart, along with Bill Forrester's, when she told them that she would be heading to Cornell for the new term. Just as soon as Prof. Revere could get everything arranged, she would begin the transfer.

CHAPTER 18 – DAY 25

The birds continued to die off, and there were fewer and fewer incidents. There were hardly any birds anywhere in the South Coast area, as they had died off completely. Tory was sitting with Chris at the kitchen table. They had had a couple of lovely days together. Chris had taken these days off work, which wasn't much of a problem since hardly anyone came down to the beach since the festival attack.

They were enjoying their coffee, and Tory said she had something she needed to tell him.

"Well, that sounds ominous. What's up?" Chris asked.

"Prof. Revere has asked me to assist her at Cornell, and she has offered me a free ride until I achieve my doctorate," she said, "I am going to take her up on it."

"That's wonderful news, congratulations!" Chris was practically bursting with pride for Tory.

"It means I will be moving to New York and I won't have any time between terms. I'll be assisting Prof. Revere with her projects, so we won't have any time to see each other," explained Tory.

"What it means is that I will finally get to see another part of the U.S.," he chuckled. "Besides after the craziness of what happened here, I think it is time I finally give some careful thought as to my career. I have decided I don't want to continue much longer as a lifeguard. So I am doing a little soul-searching myself. I am leaning toward going back into medicine. Besides, this is an outstanding opportunity for you, and I know how much you like and respect Prof. Revere."

Chris just said everything Tory hoped she would hear, but never for a moment truly expected. She jumped up and hugged his neck.

"Of course, I do expect you to finish out the summer here with your project for the zoo, as I may not be quite ready to see you leave yet," he said after she released him.

"Naturally, besides I am sure it will take some time to get all the paperwork transferred along with finding new housing and the like," said Tory beaming now.

The doorbell rang, and Chris just looked at Tory and shrugged. He got up and walked to the front door where Dr. Forrester and Prof. Revere stood smiling.

He opened the screen door and let them in saying, "Well this is an unexpected, but pleasant surprise."

"We figured you both might be here," said Prof. Revere. "We have some news to share."

"Do we have a vaccine?" said Tory unable to withhold her excitement.

Dr. Forrester produced a holder containing a dozen vials and said, "May we introduce the McKnight Super Aviary Rabies Vaccine which reverses and destroys the Aviary Rabies Virus. We are on our way over to Saddleback to turn it over to Dr. Friedman and the CDC."

"Congratulations, Tory, you came up with the answer," finished Prof. Revere.

Since Chris was closest, he grabbed and hugged Tory congratulating her in the process. Then both Dr. Forrester and Prof. Revere did the same.

"Can you tell me about it?" asked Tory wanting to know the details.

"How about over a celebratory dinner this evening?" said Dr. Forrester, "We have a lot of sick people waiting for this, including Natalie, and we need them to produce a lot more than we could at the university."

"Understood and that sounds lovely," Tory said enthusiastically, "Although I don't know how I will make it that long."

Dr. Forrester laughed and said, "Well I suggest you go ahead and start celebrating and we will have to do our best later to catch up with you. After all, it is not every day they name a cure after you. You are going to have a lot of jealous students upon your return to class."

Tory looked at Dr. Forrester and said sheepishly, "Dr. Forrester, I need to talk to you about that as well..."

"Ellen already told me," said Dr. Forrester and then quickly asked, "Does Chris know?" After both Chris and Tory nodded he continued, "Well while I am sorry to see you leave, but I couldn't be happier for you and you will now most assuredly end up as one of the top people in our field."

Tory blushed, and a tear of joy fell from her eye. Chris said, "Well, you best get that over there, as we have a great deal to celebrate!"

They said goodbye and Dr. Forrester and Prof. Revere got into Dr. Forrester's car and headed off to the medical center.

Chris said, "I don't know about you, but perhaps we could begin the celebration where we started this morning?"

Tory was still beaming and said to him teasing, "That's all you men think about, but yes, I think that would be a terrific way to start celebrating."

She took his hand and led him back to bed.

Later that day they met at a steakhouse in Dana Point that Dr. Forrester said he had wanted to try. Even before being seated, Tory began grilling them about the research and how they created the vaccine.

Prof. Revere became the spokesperson with Dr. Forrester's urging. She began, "Well we withdrew blood from the three birds before injecting them with the pathogen. After the injection, we took the samples and mixed it with the blood from a live infected bird we had obtained from the Marines. We witnessed the blood from the pelicans almost immediately form offensive T-cells against the pathogen."

Since Chris was a paramedic, he was able to follow along.

Dr. Forrester decided to explain the fundamental principle of the vaccine just in case, "As you know, there are two major kinds of lymphocytes, T-cells, and B-cells, and they each do their jobs in fighting off infection. T-cells function either offensively or defensively. The offensive T-cells don't attack the microbe directly, but they use chemical weapons to eliminate the cells that were already infected. Because they have been "programmed" by their exposure to the microbe's antigen, these cytotoxic T-cells, also called killer T-cells, can sense diseased cells that are harboring the bacterium. The killer T-cells latch onto these cells and release chemicals that destroy the infected cells and the microbes inside.

B-cells then kick in and create antibodies. These work by first grabbing onto the microbe's antigen, and then sticking to and coating the microbe. Antibodies and antigens fit together and bind to each other in one solid cell. These antibodies also work with other defensive molecules that circulate in the blood, called complement proteins, to destroy microbes."

"And as you know, the goal of most vaccines is to stimulate this response. In fact, many infectious microbes can be defeated by antibodies alone, without any help from killer T-cells. This began almost immediately in the pelican's blood, so we think they might have been predisposed to this virus or a type of it before." said Prof. Revere.

"Are you suggesting that pelicans were exposed to the aviary rabies pathogen before this incident?" asked Tory.

"Possibly as far back as Bodega Bay, or even before

that," said Dr. Forrester.

"This from the man who thought it was an urban myth," chuckled Tory.

Dr. Forrester smiled and shrugged, "Always room for new information and to change your mind."

"So they were predisposed to immunity from the virus?" Chris asked.

"It would seem, so we were able to use a weakened form of the rabies virus that would not be strong enough to keep multiplying. Then borrowing T-cells from the pelicans, we were able to create a stronger vaccine than the mammalian rabies vaccine created from the B-cells of humans," said Prof. Revere.

"And how is Natalie?" asked Chris.

"Well she'd rather be here with us right now," said Dr. Forrester, "But she is under observation to see how quickly the vaccine can combat the disease. She will make a full recovery. In fact, they estimate 80 percent of the patients they are treating with the new vaccine will make it all the way back."

"That leaves 20 percent or around one hundred people that won't," said Tory.

"Unfortunately, the rabies was too advanced for them," Prof. Revere said sadly, "But think how many more would have died if not for you, Tory."

"Think of it Tory, your name mentioned in the same breath as Louis Pasteur!" said Dr. Forrester.

"Did he develop the original rabies vaccine?" asked Chris.

"Back in 1885, he saved a young boy who had been

bitten by a rabid dog," answered Dr. Forrester. "Pasteur had been working on a rabies vaccine for several years before and had recently cured infected animals in his laboratory. By promptly administering the young boy this new, and then-untested vaccine, Pasteur saved the child's life and turned rabies into a treatable disease."

"Wow," said Chris, "That's amazing."

"Let's hope it never has to be used again like it will be in San Clemente," said Tory.

"We are working on a strain for the other birds too," said Dr. Forrester. "It will be under joint research between Cornell and SDSU. We would like to ask you to join us on that project."

Chris said, "Well, there goes the rest of our summer."

Tory asked Dr. Forrester, "What about my current project with the zoological society?"

"They completely understand that this takes precedence and they only ask that if you have more information that you submit it before starting this, otherwise you are released from that project," answered Dr. Forrester.

"It only makes sense that you would participate on your vaccine," added Prof. Revere, "And I am sorry Chris, if this interferes with your hopes and plans, especially as you know Tory will be moving to New York this August."

Chris nodded and said, "Hey, this is for the good of mankind, and if we had this sooner, perhaps a lot more people like Andy and Rachel would still be enjoying their summer rather than losing their life as they did."

"Unfortunately that is true," said Prof. Revere, "But at least we might be able to prevent it from ever happening again."

"You know, we could always use a medical student in our research," said Dr. Forrester to Chris, "Your experience and medical background might be beneficial in all this."

Chris instantly perked up and said, "I was entertaining the idea of getting further in my medical degree. San Diego might not be too bad. Let me give it some thought. Perhaps I can work out some weekday lodging somewhere."

"I might have an idea on that," said Tory, and they all laughed.

Dr. Forrester offered to help Chris get back in the mainstream at SDSU and their medical program. "Especially as I will have one less student taking up all of my time," he said playfully at Tory.

They talked about the future, ideas and further hopes. Everyone at the table had relaxed for the first time in weeks.

The waiter brought their dinner, and they all settled into their plates. They all gave thanks secretly that the return of the birds was finally conquered, and hoped that with their combined help, it would never happen again.

The End

EPILOGUE

As everyone was celebrating the end of the danger that had ensued, more than a dozen California gulls were flying north to their summer nesting grounds. The gulls held a protected status because of previous declining numbers at their historic California breeding colony at Mono Lake. But recently the gulls were successfully breeding in the southern portion of San Francisco Bay. Current years had seen these birds undergo an exponential population growth. California gulls now inhabit large, remote salt-production ponds and levees and have a tremendous food sources provided by nearby landfills from San Francisco and its suburbs, all the way up into Sacramento.

In fact, this colony had grown from less than 1,000 breeding birds in 1982 to well over 33,000 early in the 21st century. The population boom resulted in large flocks of gulls opportunistically preying on other species, especially their eggs and nestlings. It had become a source of heated debate in the California capitol. As these birds headed north, two camps, one for the continuing protection of these birds and one for pulling their protective status, raged on in Sacramento.

These particular birds had been foraging in flight and picked up food while swimming, walking or wading around Southern California. On their migration pattern, the flock made a stop in San Clemente a couple days before. The gulls found scraps of meat from the dead birds floating around the pier. They ate their fill before moving on up the coast.

As they continued their flight, their appetites seemed to grow. It would take another full week before they would reach the massive breeding grounds. Many of these gulls had already successfully mated in this group and were anxious to get to their large colony to build nests and feed on the nestlings of other birds. A solitary thought grew in their minds as they flew. Got to eat. Got to eat.

About The Author

Joe Moore has written millions of words over his lifetime. A graduate from California State University, Northridge, Joe is a former publisher, editor, advertising, marketing and sales executive. He worked on hundreds of campaigns and articles with thousands of proposals and stories for everything from fishing equipment to business magazines. This may help explain why he is able to write in so many genres.

Moore was a former feature writer for several Southern California periodicals. He has three books published in his **Santa Claus Trilogy** – *Believe Again, The North Pole Chronicles and Faith, Hope & Reindeer and Glaciers Melt & Mountains Smoke.* He is very excited to have several children's books also published. *Santa's World Introducing Santa's Elf Series, Jamie Hardrock, Chief Mining Elf, Shelley Wrapitup, Master Design Elf, Keeney Eagleye, Naughty/Nice List Manager, Sarah Buttons, Master Doll Maker and Ford MacHarley, Master Wheelsmith* all for Santa's Elf Series©. These books are produced for early readers, written in rhyme, and illustrated by Moore's wife, Mary. Moore has written over a dozen children's stories for the Santa's Elf Series that will be published at the rate of two per year.

Moore has been seen and interviewed on nearly every news program, such as Good Morning America, Fox News, ABC/NBC/CBS News and in numerous radio programs and newspapers. He also appeared on Disney Surfers, Nickelodeon, in numerous parades, on billboards and he and his wife were featured guests on

Wealth TV with the late Charlie Jones (NFL Media Hall of Fame announcer). As a professional Santa Claus, he currently is the premiere Santa Claus for Hello Santa digital Santa visits and works with daycare centers, visited dozens of homes and corporations, and spread his goodwill and joy with Mrs. Claus everywhere they travel.

Joe and Mary Moore, (as Santa and Mrs. Claus) also give of themselves, having contributed countless hours (and toys) to worthy charities including, the American Cancer Society, Children's Hospitals, Military families, Domestic abuse shelters, Community projects for schools, "Angel" programs, Hospice centers and more. Both Joe & Mary feel truly blessed by God to be able to bring such joy and happiness to others.

Moore's other passion is cooking! He enjoys creating spectacular meals for Mary and his friends. He also enjoys fishing, even though he admits his wife can always out fish him!

The Moores reside in the beautiful Smoky Mountains of East Tennessee.